T0207889

FOUNDING FATHER
OF THE
TWENTY-FIRST
CENTURY

FOUNDING FATHER
—— OF THE ——
TWENTY-FIRST
CENTURY

The Presidential Memoir of Henderson West,
Forty-Fifth President of the United States of America

KENNETH JACKSON

FOUNDING FATHER OF THE TWENTY-FIRST CENTURY
THE PRESIDENTIAL MEMOIR OF HENDERSON WEST,
FORTY-FIFTH PRESIDENT OF THE UNITED STATES OF
AMERICA

iUniverse books may be ordered through booksellers or by contacting:

iUniverse
1663 Liberty Drive
Bloomington, IN 47403
www.iuniverse.com
1-800-Authors (1-800-288-4677)

Because of the dynamic nature of the Internet, any web addresses or links contained in this book may have changed since publication and may no longer be valid. The views expressed in this work are solely those of the author and do not necessarily reflect the views of the publisher, and the publisher hereby disclaims any responsibility for them.

Any people depicted in stock imagery provided by Thinkstock are models, and such images are being used for illustrative purposes only. Certain stock imagery © Thinkstock.

ISBN: 978-1-5320-0061-4 (sc)
ISBN: 978-1-5320-0062-1 (e)

Print information available on the last page.

iUniverse rev. date: 08/05/2016

Contents

FOREWORD

IT'S 2050. WHY NOW?

Remembering back these 30-plus years to inauguration day on Friday, January 20, 2017, I will state, for the first time ever, that I was not only disturbed but genuinely unhappy with my situation. There I was, Henderson West, publicly-recognized poster-child for disillusionment with institutional America, yet now the head of it all.

I had grown up at the end of the twentieth century, willing to challenge any formal organization, public institution, existing modern mindset or "ism." I was hardly an anarchist, however, and I was a huge supporter of individual freedom, but there is no way I would have seen myself as part of the process at the time. I had prided my personal successes on the ability to work-around bureaucratic processes, rather than by immersing myself in them.

I was a successful businessman who had accumulated billions. I wouldn't say I was disillusioned at all regarding that part of America. My financial success had been simply a matter of hard work, open-mindedness, good vision and, of course, a bit of good luck. My company, NutrisHouse, had become a globally recognized business leader.

Personal success aside, I will just be blunt: I was anti-government in most of its forms at the start of the 21st century. In fact, the hallmark of my success had been the ability to manage governmental process and obstacles. I earned a reputation as someone who did not listen to governmental authority and on many occasions outright ignored regulation if a greater good was impeded. Government, I believed, was equally inept everywhere. In 2017, the USA's government was the worst in the developed world, involving itself primarily in the pursuit of self-interest and party politics. The Republican and Democratic parties postured and opposed each other in order to undermine the authority of whichever party, at the time, happened to have won the previous election. Government was an elitist system that fostered the interests of the party, select business interests and the wealthy. As my own public record at the time shows, I had no interest in politics and contributed nothing of my personal energy or corporate finances to it.

If you had told me, on my 46th birthday, March 2nd, 2016, that I, Henderson West, was going to be the next president and that, 35 years later my name would be synonymous with George Washington, Abraham Lincoln or Thomas Jefferson, I would have thought you to be the dumbest person I had ever met. Further, to be referred to across America as the "founding father of the twenty-first century" or ff21st for short, would have been beyond even the realm of my imagination. In fact, becoming president would likely have been the worst thing I could imagine.

This is why I was genuinely confused and irritated on Friday, January 20th of 2017, as I was being sworn in as the 45th President of the United States of America. I sincerely did not want the role and was wondering why I had just ruined my life.

Most former presidents write their memoirs shortly after their term is over. You might wonder why I chose to wait so long. Well, I put it like this: was I more comfortable trying to write about my time as president or was I going to write a more complete memoir that incorporated a long-term view and took into consideration others people's thoughts? Not to disparage any of my presidential predecessors, but evaluating one's actions too soon is an arrogant undertaking. Even now, in 2050, I still feel uncomfortable trying to write about my time as president.

But, here goes.

CHAPTER 1

APRIL 15, 2016...I COULD HAVE DIED, INSTEAD I BECAME PRESIDENT

So, how did a 46-year-old business man who didn't like anything about our political system become president? The day that changed my life was Friday, April 15th, 2016. The day that I was shot. As per normal when getting shot, there was no foreshadowing that this day would be any different than any other.

I was scheduled to give a speech at the New York Metropolitan Museum as part of a fund-raiser for a local charity group. At the time I was deeply involved with my own benevolent foundations that had gained some notoriety due to my direct "on-the-ground" approach to solving humanitarian issues. While today it might appear hypocritical that I was a keynote speaker at a traditional fund-raiser at the Met, in 2016 it was ground-breaking. My attendance was designed to convince other charitable organizations that their efforts would be more effective if they focused on implementation programs rather than simply providing a monetary contribution or fund-raising.

The gala started at six in the evening. I was scheduled to arrive at six-thirty and I was to leave by nine.

My day had been routine when I got to the museum. Millie Scotts, my assistant, had coordinated the day perfectly. The weather had stayed true to form and had reached 72 degrees by mid-afternoon and the city was in one of those consummate New York moods when everyone felt on top of the world and happy to be alive. People were out riding bikes, walking their dogs, lounging in the patio bars, and tourists were walking in droves along 5th Avenue. But on that day, pedestrian traffic did seem to be moving at a more relaxed pace than usual. I had only been bumped into three or four times when it should have been into the hundreds after covering as much ground as I had.

I was feeling joyful the entire day and one of my colleagues had even commented on my smile several times. It got to the point where I had to ask if he thought I was never happy. I guess I had a bit of a reputation for being a jerk on occasion. Perhaps cheerfulness was just not one of my primary characteristics in 2016. Anyway, appearing to be happy all the time, as many people aspire too, is a bit unrealistic.

Happiness is more about purpose and accomplishment than a simple smile.

I was a product of the "more, more, more" culture as much as anyone else, and perhaps more than most. I of course am aware that accumulating as much wealth as I had made me appear as if I were striving to just have more. I readily admit that the accumulation of wealth is sometimes simply about getting more. It is addictive.

In the late 20th century, the pursuit of happiness was linked directly to increased consumption, one of the biggest schisms between reality and fantasy in the history of American culture. There was an inherent paradox that an individual was always striving to be happy but could never attain it as you forever needed more "goods" for fulfillment. This is why hardly anyone was genuinely happy, except of course for the companies that made anti-depressant pharmaceuticals.

With hindsight firmly in play, I do acknowledge that there is a big difference between positivity and happiness. Positivity is more about a forward-looking optimism, which I always embraced, while happiness strikes me as a more in-the-moment enthusiasm. Today I try to focus on the moment and revel in the enthusiasm while continuing to sustain my on-going positivity and optimism for the future.

I still, however, do not smile very much.

But back to the day I was shot.

When we arrived at the Met, the sun was bright on the horizon. As usual, Millie and I were in the limo and we were directed to the vehicle queue in front of the Met. In front of my car was another vehicle carrying my security detail. I had never gotten used to having security. I certainly never felt myself as a target for any reason. As a billionaire it was just expected that I would have security, but deep down I always wondered who would try to hurt me?

This feeling was born out of two separate, but equally misguided attitudes.

The first was simply my own arrogance that I was just too important or too rich to have someone take a shot at me. Who, I thought, could penetrate my world and get into my personal space? I used to move about quite freely, and without security, no matter where I was. I rarely stayed in my hotel room when I was overseas. I considered myself much less recognizable while traveling and I would on occasion just wander off by myself and explore the cities or museums.

When I was in the USA, I was home. At home is where you are supposed to feel the most safe and secure. When I look back at the gun-related violence of the times, I cannot for the life of me understand what was in my mind.

The second attitude I possessed, which strikes me as very counter-intuitive to the first, was my own perceived sense of unimportance. I was just an unassuming guy who was trying to get along with everyone and make the world a better place. Why would anyone want to hurt me? Yet I always knew there were people out there who neither liked me personally nor appreciated what I represented.

For example, I had done a profile in *Forbes* magazine and had been vilified for my personal style, and my willingness to forgo regulations. The article high-lighted a litany of my business mistakes in a very embarrassing manner and portrayed me as a blundering fool. I was shocked that someone would write an article that had nothing good to say about my business practices. Another example was the health care business community who felt I was a demon incarnate for my ability to shift people's thinking towards preventive medicine rather than diagnosis and treatment. As a result, I must have cost that sector billions over the years. I could understand why I had no enthusiastic supporters in some business realms, but on a personal level, I never felt I had an enemies.

Finally, and I still really hate to acknowledge this, but there are people in the world who dislike you just for existing. In 2016, there were many folks that were members of disenfranchised parts of America, factions of society that were anti-capitalism and anti-wealth. Whether these views stemmed from religion, ideology or insanity, is irrelevant. The bottom-line was that there were indeed American citizens who viewed me as their enemy and to them, it was very personal. Even today in 2050, there are many people out there who dislike me, but fortunately not as many as there used to be.

By 6:15 my security personnel were on the sidewalk. My security detail that April was very different from what I received when I became president. The secret service were fanatics compared to my people. My people were in no way incompetent, just not as well-trained or as zealous. And I would have never paid for all the pre-inspections, crowd monitoring and protective positioning that would have thwarted the attack. I do not hold them accountable and never have.

Before Millie had gotten out of the car, she instructed me as to where the photo and TV cameras were set-up. Doing the "red carpet" was of course part of the drill. Getting your picture on TV and in the newspaper was often the whole point of having the fund-raiser in the first place.

I waited in the car for another thirty seconds, which was when Millie tossed her handbag over her shoulder – our established cue that everything is wide-open and the cameras ready to go. It didn't take very long for the photographers and the crowd to get focused on my car.

I remember the next six minutes vividly.

I stepped onto the red carpet, leaned out of the car and stood up straight. Millie had moved slightly to the left behind the car to be out of camera-view. She hated having her picture taken with me in these environments for it made her feel inconsequential. She preferred to step aside. I also noticed over her shoulder, to the left, a throng of people who were cordoned off. There were maybe four hundred people, fans trying to do some celebrity gazing and maybe get an autograph. To the right was the red carpet area where the cameras were.

I waved to the crowd and they gave me a rather large and respectful round of applause. At this time I was more of a notable type of celebrity rather than a real star. Your average reaction would have been: "Look, that's Henderson West over there. You know the super rich guy." Or, something to that effect. Your friend would then go, "Oh, so it is." That was usually it. Unless you were a business person who would like to try to get involved with my company, there really wasn't much interest beyond that. I was perfectly fine with this arrangement. All I ever wanted from notoriety was to be able to cut the line at a restaurant on occasion.

As I got out of the car, I executed my one and only move that I felt was a kind of celebrity-oriented. I took two steps forward so that the car door could be closed, then I quickly reached up and grabbed my jacket lapels and gave them a solid downward shrug. It kind of looked like an unorthodox adjustment but to me it was just an amusing way to get the tiniest reaction. It had become my trademark move. However, after I became president, almost everyone in the world had seen this move and there probably was a period during the height of my popularity when most folks did it over and over themselves. There were, in fact, many memes and videos at the time of people replicating my jacket adjustment technique. The influence of pop culture can be over-whelming and befuddling.

I smiled and waved for a few more seconds then I turned to the right and was greeted by the chairperson for the evening's events. I shook her hand, bowed formally to her then gave her a light kiss on the cheek.

I was introduced to several dignitaries and members of the organizing committee and we exchanged cordial greetings. I remember just how informal the whole process seemed to be. Despite the formality of the clothing and the red carpet, it struck me that the organizers and guests were in a very relaxed mood. The crowd itself was appreciative and jovial. I couldn't help thinking just how much better life was when the sun was out and how great it would be to capture that feeling and make it available to everyone, all the time. Ironic that I would have this thought just moments before someone tries to kill me.

When I got to the photographers' area, my security were in front of me facing the cameras. I smiled and waved until Millie grabbed me by the elbow and directed me toward the first of three TV interviews.

When I finished my first interview, I noticed a slight disturbance in the crowd, like a fight had broken out and that the crowd was simply separating a bit to let the combatants go at it. Now being someone who had been around the world a few times, someone who had seen photographers grappling for position which occasionally turned hostile, I didn't think too much of it. I did think that there really was no reason for anyone to get pushed around while jostling to get a picture of me. I do recall Millie's grip ever so slightly tightening on my arm while tugging me to the next interview.

The movement in the crowd however was just enough for me to linger longer than I normally would have, and that is when I saw the man, who I would later find out was named Nicholas

Zahan, staring at me. He had a furrowed brow and a vacant look in his eyes. His hair was catching the sun and falling and flitting so uniformly. It struck me as a perfect hairstyle, something I should try out. Then the gun barrel cut through the path of sunlight. It really did not register that I might be in danger, though upon seeing the gun, I looked into his eyes to see what was going through his mind and what he was might be trying to do. His eyes were definitely locked on mine.

When the gun barrel settled on me, the barrel was all I saw. Everything else faded into the background. I remember that heightened sense of awareness, and it provided me a sense of purpose and may have even been a spirit of providence that allowed the actions that followed. I have never had that feeling again.

As dumb as it sounds, I was still not aware that I was the target, but having seen the gun I obviously knew that something bad was about to happen. My only instinct was to jump into the situation. It never occurred to me that I could die nor was there any sense of heroism in order to try and "save the day." It was just the way I reacted.

By this time, Mr. Zahan was only three feet from the barricade so rather than move directly towards the gun, I went for his left shoulder. I had noticed a drawstring on his hoodie and this was what I reached for.

I dove over the barricade and lunged toward him. There was no thought of "let's simply wrestle the gun away"; the best way to end the situation was to render the attacker incapacitated.

As I rammed into him, I was bringing my left arm up to force his arm into the air so, at a minimum, if any shots went off they would go up rather than at me or anyone else. I was also trying to immobilize his arms and I figured that I might be able to strip the gun from his outstretched hand.

I definitely heard all three shots. Many people ask how I didn't know that I had taken a bullet to the left shoulder. I don't really know how to explain this, as I didn't realize that I had been hit until after the man had been wrestled to the ground and detained by NYC police. I did feel a bit of soreness in my shoulder area, but it was more like a tender muscle than a gunshot wound.

Adrenalin has the tremendous ability to help your mind decide what you need to focus on. I saw a gun and instantly realized my life or maybe someone else's was in danger so I simply sprang into action. I feel that being aware of a bullet in my shoulder would have proven to be a distraction from the task at hand, which was survival for me and the protection of others. I guess I have been gifted with a calm, rational mind that allows me to stay in the moment and yet be proactive, especially under chaotic circumstances.

For example, I once hydroplaned on the highway. As I started skidding my mind went through a series of observations regarding where we were headed and where I should to try to steer the car. There was an embankment to the right and a guard rail to the left so I attempted to steer the car into the guard rail. Fortunately, the car swung around and the rear fender rammed the guard rail and rode it down the highway until we came to a stop pinned to the railing.

There was another time when I was a teenager where I had been hit by a car while crossing a street. I hit the ground, winded, but had the wherewithal to pull myself onto the median so that I was out of the traffic and off the road.

On another occasion, I found myself perched on the side of a snowy cliff in the Rockies without any ropes and knowing that my friends did not know where I was. I was not a very experienced rock climber and I knew that I could die easily in this situation, two hundred feet above the nearest snow drift. I considered jumping to the drift and I felt that even though I would then be rescued, I would likely injure myself quite severely. I wasn't quite ready to take that chance.

I surveyed my surroundings and the only route out was a 15 foot climb to the top ridge. That may not seem like much to experienced climbers, but it felt like miles to me. I would also have to make a four foot jump onto a very narrow ledge in order to get to the first foothold. I knew that I would have to jump. If I fell, so be it. I set to work determining what my best approach was. How hard I would need to push, what were the areas that I could grab with my hands and if the landing area was clear or icy. To lessen the physical burden, I decided to leave my backpack behind.

Then I simply went ahead and made the jump and climbed up to safety. The whole situation only lasted ten minutes, but it was a testament to my level-headed approach even in what are considered emergency conditions. (By the way, I went back later in the day to try to retrieve my backpack but I could not get at it, so it is likely still there.)

As a result of these and other circumstances, I had always felt confident that I would handle any emergency or crisis situation very well. In hindsight, my bigger problem was avoiding the situations in the first place.

The final thing I do recall, and this is what most people remember, is that I punched the shooter after I rammed into him, cocked my right arm as he was falling and delivered a punch that hit him squarely on the jaw. Several by-standers and my security people then jumped on Mr. Zahan.

During his trial, Mr. Zahan expressed regret for his actions, saying he could not even comprehend why he had done it or why I was the target. He had a typical delinquent biography at the time. A disillusioned youth, no financial success, problems with authority, a drug addiction and a poor family history. It was the frequent scenario of the alienated transgressor in the early 21st century. His lawyers made him out to be just another societal casualty, which, to be honest, did bother me significantly during the trial.

Personally, I like to think that I hit him so hard it knocked some sense into him.

Millie Scotts was the only other casualty of the day, as the second shot had grazed her arm when she had rushed to my aid. She had tried to pull me from the fray but had inadvertently moved herself into the line of fire and she got hit. The first bullet went into my shoulder and the third one ended up in a tree across the walk way. We both recovered very quickly and both consider ourselves lucky to have survived with such minor injuries. April 15th, 2016, could easily have been the end of me.

The shooting resulted in two important movements, neither of which I could have expected. The first was the terrific ground swell of support for me personally and my increased notoriety, and the second was a shift of my core thinking.

Of course the altercation became a story all over the world. The video of Zahan pulling out his gun, me jumping at him, the gun discharging, the "punch of sanity" as it became known, and finally the gun being knocked from his hands was shown over and over for weeks. To this day I am still stunned by what a media stir it caused. All the USA news shows went into their 24 hour coverage, as did the BBC, CNA, South American and African news channels. At the time, YouTube was the predominant video site on the internet and within a week the video had been seen over ten million times. By the end of 2016, fueled by my run for the presidency, it had over one billion views.

Why did this story capture so much attention and generate so much good will toward me? I was not the first person to be shot, but I was certainly one of the wealthiest. It was not the act of getting shot that was interesting, but that I reacted and subdued the shooter. A spark of self-reliance and fierceness was ignited. Essentially, I suddenly became a better alternative than Donald Trump for those who had become alienated with the direction America was headed. Where Trump had limited and polarizing appeal, I was able to gain enthusiastic wide spread support.

In 2016, the majority of Americans were tired of feeling beat upon. The early 21ˢᵗ century was an exasperating period. There was the mortgage crisis and subsequent recession, the poor economy, the growth of China as an international power, the collapse of the American dollar, the Ebola scare, natural disasters like Hurricane Katrina and the Gulf Coast tsunami, the consolidation of wealth, the war in the Middle East, 9/11, the rise of domestic terrorism and the fear of Islam. Let's not forget the overall ineffective US political system and the poor performances of Presidents Bush and Obama. By 2016, hope was lacking in many quarters of American society and change looked impossible. Americans saw my actions as one man standing up for himself and literally fighting back to defend his life.

Until my election, most Americans had begrudgingly accepted the political and economic system. They felt they had no recourse in this time of need. The government, the banks, the medical community, the legal system, Wall Street and the real estate sector were not benefiting them. It was not only lost faith, but a genuine recognition that these systems existed to benefit the elite and that, in the process, these institutions were causing serious harm to the average citizen. People found themselves without direction.

The "West's Punch of Sanity" video filled a void and offered an alternative solution.

My punch reawakened the spirit of what it really was to be an American. By that I mean this: You do not just let things happen to you and then be done with it and walk away with your tail hanging between your legs. Americans fight back as individuals and as a nation to establish their position. This was the public movement that propelled me into the White House.

I mentioned earlier that there was a second aspect of the shooting that affected my core beliefs.

I had always been an empathetic person and I tried very hard, most of the time, to understand the other person's point of view and the context of their situation. As many people will recall, I was sympathetic towards Mr. Zahan shortly after the shooting. In fact, I went on record stating that I hoped he did not get any prison time. Like so many, I was consumed with politically-correct thinking and the willingness to blame society as an excuse for an individual's deviant behavior.

However, I started to get very indignant that both I and Mr. Zahan lived in a nation that he felt had given him the right to end my life without any type of provocation. This definition of freedom was one that that I could no longer accept. Until the shooting, I did not hold many restrictions in regard to individual freedom and genuinely felt that anyone could do pretty much whatever they wanted. After hearing though, what the defense put forth during the trial it became pretty clear to me that actions should have more severe consequences. Further, the ease which people were willing to absolve themselves of responsibility for their actions at the mortal expense of another, seemed downright immoral. This is the point in my life where I started wholeheartedly developing the thinking that became the rallying cries of personal responsibility: the notion of "personal contribution." Personal contribution as we know now in 2050 is the hallmark for the determination of personal valuation and the subsequent societal rewards. Over time, my thoughts became more crystallized and as a result this was the foundation of a new America, and the moment when we started to regain strength and power.

This is the period whereby the USA in my mind regained its conscience. Why should a society exist where someone who has contributed virtually nothing, as in the case of Mr. Zahan, have the right to kill someone who has employed thousands of people, curtailed world hunger and increased the health and lifespan of Americans?

The foundation of my thinking was that those individuals who make the greatest contribution to their field should reap the greatest returns in terms of power, leadership and of course financial reward. The second premise was that there needed to be a shift in what was considered a rewarding field. For example, successful Hollywood people can make millions of dollars for entertaining American children while successful teachers make tens of thousands for teaching them. Wall Street traders make millions or even billions of dollars while scientists make a fraction of that. There were so many examples at the turn of the century that the list was simply endless.

As the corollary premise then, those who made the least contribution should not expect to receive much beyond basic sustenance. Those who chose to contribute very little or thought that life owed them a living, were soon to find out that America owed them nothing.

America should be first and foremost about individual freedom. However, societal influence should be obtained through societal contribution.

My goal was never, nor will it ever be to dictate the income, power or leadership that any individual could attain but rather to have society at large play a greater role in determining what roles are worthy of substantive financial rewards. Does a baseball player deserve to make five million dollars while a fireman makes fifty thousand dollars? Many Americans today of course believe in complete free markets and say yes due to their belief in absolute freedom and the free market. It will sound contradictory, but I agree with these principals as well. What I set out to do in office though, was to have the market and society change the definition of freedom to personal responsibility and embrace a free market where ethics, values and contribution were considered the most valuable characteristics of successful people. Individuals are still free to do what they want, but in terms of societal privilege there are now a great many economic sectors whereby the only reward you will enjoy is money.

So, on to my election story.

The popular movement that led me to become president was exhilarating. I was very resistant to the idea if not completely against it in the days following the shooting. My initial thoughts were guided by just how much I hated the political system of our country.

I had of course watched in 2008 while President Obama ran his campaign. I was indeed an enthusiastic observer and wished for nothing less than Mr. Obama to win and bring about the sweeping reformations and institutional changes he claimed. However, by his second election win in 2012, I had lost complete faith in him and our government overall. For all the enthusiasm I might have held during the fall of 2008, I was equally as disenfranchised in the spring of 2016. As he entered the final year of his term in 2016, due to the many transgressions against the privacy of American citizens, the rise of international terrorism, the inability to deal with immigration reform, the continued spiraling national debt and his inability to manage Congress, my alienation with the American government was at its deepest point ever.

What troubled me the most during Mr. Obama's presidency, was just how little influence the president's position actually had. Upon his inauguration in 2009, President Obama had a vision that was shared by many Americans, but the institutions of government seemed too convoluted and dysfunctional for any progress to be made.

President George W. Bush prior to President Obama had had similar obstacles, but was still able to move programs forward. Now in all candor, many programs that Bush developed and moved forward were done so by usurping the democratic principles on which the country was founded. His government struck me as more autocratic than democratic. Either way, whether discussing Presidents Obama or Bush, the bottom line was that the United States government was extremely ineffective and dare I say meaningless to the majority of Americans. It was this cultural antipathy that fueled the momentum of my campaign.

One of the things I love most about the USA is our constant ability to strive to do the right thing. This has been a hallmark of freedom since our inception. Our founding fathers set out to create an entire new world, one where individual goals and personal achievements would result in the greatest rewards and individual autonomy. At its core, they strove for a merit system rather than a hereditary one. To be fair, in our pursuit of an ideal meritocracy, there have been many examples of overt hypocrisy and downright immorality. Slavery, usurpation of freedom, government misrepresentation and even assassinations have shown that America does not always live up to its own values. But these atrocities of government are counter-balanced by a desire by some (quite often not very many in the beginning) to abolish them, punish the perpetrators and finally rise up in disgust over the unethical acts of government. The wonder of America is that even though there have been gross violations of humanity, our vision is never abandoned and our nation and people ultimately embrace an appropriate course of action. Righteousness prevails.

By 2016, a pent up personal dissatisfaction coupled with a wide-held disillusionment towards government and society allowed a fellow like me to come to the presidency. Trust was lacking. Corruption, lobbying, cronyism and devious policy were systemic. American citizens and the global community were against the USA more so than at any other time in our history. I feel I was quite simply seen as a symbol of integrity, a trait that had diminished significantly not only in government, but in most aspects of American society.

The definitive moment for me to actually make the decision to run for president was on May 4th of 2016, when John Kasich abandoned his run for the Republican nomination. Ted Cruz had abandoned his campaign one day earlier and this left Donald Trump as the presumptive nominee. The thing that scared me the most was that he might actually win the presidency. I figured Mr. Trump would prove to be an entertaining character and bring some interesting rhetoric to the process, which of course he did and went far beyond anyone's imagination. However, his support levels continued to grow and grow. When he entered the race in 2015, I never dreamed that he would win the nomination, but now he pretty much had it. It didn't seem all that unrealistic anymore to me that he could be the president.

Donald Trump's success however, represented something fantastic to me. The desire for significant change by Americans. Mr. Trump was clearly an outsider and a strong-willed candidate who was not beholding to the party system. To me, this was a great occurrence. Due to his success, I felt that I might have a genuine opportunity to win if I offered a more benevolent and completely independent platform.

This same outsider thinking was reflected as well with the Democrats.

Bernie Sanders had emerged as a legitimate voice for many Americans in opposition to the status quo candidate, Hillary Clinton. However, despite his impressive showing, the Democrats were going to put forward Hillary Clinton as their candidate during the national convention in July. She certainly was a valid candidate with years of political experience. However, to me she represented the "same old thing" in terms of being a product of a political establishment that simply did not work. That Bernie Sanders had done as well as he did was inspirational to me, and gave me a sense that with the right message, some citizens might actually gravitate to someone – like me – who was willing to challenge the system.

Finally, I just did not like the thought of another Clinton being in the White House. America is supposed to be about meritocracy not oligarchy, and with Mrs. Clinton having the potential for two terms, that could have meant that a Bush or

Clinton would have been the president for 28 of the previous 36 years. That was unacceptable to me.

Regardless of who the traditional parties were putting forward as candidates, what was obvious was that the office of the President of the United States of America was becoming irrelevant on the global stage. Domestically, as was evident in the campaigning, becoming president was simply a goal to be obtained, rather than a role for an individual to fulfill. The president's position had become merely a public relations role and a factor of an individual's popularity paired with party affiliation. Mr. Trump had certainly proven this, though the party was very unhappy with his victory.

Mrs. Clinton, I felt, was a strong candidate, but the legacy from Barack Obama's presidency was not strong enough for her to leverage. And even though Mrs. Clinton was a highly respected politician, she did not have broad enough support from the nation to be president. Sadly, her best chance was to be seen as less destructive than Donald Trump. If she won, it would simply be four more years of ineffective government.

Therefore, with the prospect of Donald Trump or Hillary Clinton being the next president, I formally decided to enter the race for President. It was June 1st, 2016, just six weeks after I was shot, and four months prior to election day on November 8th. Neither of the parties had held their national conventions yet, which to me represented the kick-off of the formal campaign. I was late to the race, but felt I had a chance.

I instituted some personal conditions on my participation. The first was that I would have not have a party affiliation. I would be 100% independent. I would not get involved with any of the Congressional elections and I would not establish an election committee nor try to organize the electorate. There were two reasons for this: 1) I really did not have time and 2) I wasn't even sure I wanted to win. I did of course welcome anyone in the USA who wanted to pitch in and who held the spirit of public service in their heart. If they wanted to offer support, I encouraged them to run for office and to do what they wanted locally. However, I refused any offer of financial campaign support or endorsements.

At the time, this was considered crazy. Financial contribution had become the backbone of the American political system, and to attempt to run for office without sizable contribution was a fool's venture. For example, in 2014, during the mid-term elections a record $6.4 billion had been spent by the candidates, parties and various interested Americans. It reeked of commerce rather than democracy. This year though, it seemed that money had less influence. Jeb Bush was easily defeated despite having party support and the deep pockets of wealthy Republicans. Sanders and Trump were also not relying heavily on donations.

If local groups wanted to raise funds, that was their right. I was not going to spend much of my own money and I was not willing to dig myself into debt by accepting funds. A couple of super-pacs supported me, but I did not encourage them nor did I entertain any discussions with them. It turned out that most of them were against me anyway. I planned to campaign the old fashion way and just stump around the country, make good speeches, meet as many people as possible and take advantage of digital media.

The formal announcement of my candidacy was held in front of the Metropolitan Museum of Art on 5ᵗʰ Avenue in New York City. I am not one to shy away from a perfectly logical spotlight. The podium was in the same spot where Mr. Zahan had shot me. The first thing I stated was that I would propose no policy platforms.

What I did actually state at the time was the following:

- I will think and work in the best interest of America;
- I will deal with each issue separately and as it materializes;
- I will accept no financial support from any source;
- The American public will be more engaged in government;

- Election to, and employment within the public sector will be effective and considered a privilege.

These five items were all I ever "stated" to do if I were elected president. I purposely chose to not use the word "promised."

Making political promises is illogical. The reality of the world in the summer of 2016 was that it was just too complex and varied to have any type of formal agenda or ideology to rely on. I marveled at just how easily candidates promised to do this or that, when they had no idea what would be involved. Important issues and events materialize out of nowhere and have no historical context (or in some instances too much). Many of these issues are inharmonious with existing doctrine or previous legislation. Therefore, approaching situations with predetermined tactics often did not work as it had earlier in history. A good example is the War in the Middle East. It was certainly escalated by America's involvement and its willingness to do things the way they always did, i.e. "Bomb the Hell out Them." I did not make claims that I would create jobs, institute health care, utilize the military, balance the budget, or democratize the world. Citizens were astounded that I made no "election-type promises." I just didn't see the point, and I considered it pandering to the American public. Besides, Mr. Trump was offering up solutions for every problem under the sun.

The third thing I "stated" not to do was accept financial contributions of any kind. This should be self-evident if you are in government. Accepting money infers debt. I did not want to be beholden to anyone.

Most financial contributions were used to exploit the media anyway. One of my pet peeves with politics in 2016 was the growth of the media and how it had become an entertainment medium and in not just a few instances a manipulator of public policy. Election periods were now running 18 months, and being in the media spotlight was the primary goal rather than governing the country. Fox News was a voice for the Republican Party and did very little to hide this considering the number of pundits who were also members of the Republican Party or the Tea Party. This offended me deeply and I vowed during my candidacy to not purposely exploit my access to the media. Since the assassination attempt I had become very much an international notable person so yes I was continually in demand for interviews. I turned down almost every request. Social media, though, I could control. I ended up with millions of followers on Twitter, Facebook, Pinterest, Instagram, Snapchat etc. Whenever the media tried to side with me for their advantage, or against me as a means of pushing their candidates and agenda, I could track, follow-up and interact in real time on social media as well as from my own website. By August I had become a global name and people all over the world were hoping that I would win the presidency.

This overt non-exposure in the traditional news media created a whole new way to get elected. People had become tired of the drawn-out election process as well as the confusing and malicious messages that were part of the process. As people became more and more engaged in the politics and democracy of the US, they also became more interested in receiving a candidate's actual views and thinking. The sound-bite format of television became obsolete.

Further, I ran a fair and honest communication platform. I made no references to any of the other candidates, which irked them both as they made constant attacks on me. I have learned over the years that the greatest way to annoy someone is to ignore what they say. Everyone when they are upset thinks that they should be listened to, and their thoughts should be countered. I of course do not hold this thought process at all, as the only person I need to be confident with is myself. My lack of response or even acknowledgment of others in the race was a clearly good tactic. I even refused to take part in any candidate debates beyond the first one. It had worked for Mr. Trump during his nomination process and I took a large risk in leaving it up to the voters to see my intentions. Fortunately, they had faith in me. That I chose to be positive throughout my communications with the American public touched a lot of nerves as well.

By 2016 many people had been hurt by the recession and were disillusioned and lacking faith in the American system. My goal was to restore faith and confidence not only in America, but in themselves. Hence my election platform: STAND UP AMERICA.

STAND UP AMERICA became a rallying cry through the latter part of 2016 as a spirit of renewal took hold. We as individuals have all been down at one time or another and the measure of any person's strength is the ability to get going again. This is the same for a nation, especially one as great as the USA. The spirit of "standing up" for one's own situation and then being responsible for improving one's personal state of affairs fueled a culture of success and hard work that led to a much more positive attitude within our borders and led to an almost immediate economic recovery.

One of the difficulties we have as Americans is the ability to admit that maybe we make mistakes or that we can occasionally let ourselves down. We had embraced a culture of blaming others and to admit that we were wrong was beyond our abilities. Well, what I recognized and shared, was that we had created our own mess through a very out-dated governmental model, a business culture that celebrated profit as the only reason for existing and a citizen base that had lost its collective American spirit. We can take this situation back to the boomer generation, who grew up with a selfish bias that destroyed many American values.

We can also refer to the terrorist attacks on September 11, 2001 when we were finally proven vulnerable. Through the balance of the following decade we allowed government and businesses to run rough-shod over individual freedoms and values for the sake of national security and economic strength. Well, history has shown the effect of these circumstances, so it was just a matter of getting individual Americans committed to the concept of freedom, and what their contribution to freedom needed to be. Not surprisingly, young Americans ultimately turned out to be the leaders in the re-emergence of America.

STAND UP AMERICA become a mantra that carried us through to today, though it is far less necessary today than in was in 2016. STAND UP AMERICA became associated with the core American values that were outlined in the Declaration of Independence and the intentions of the founding fathers. Freedom is not a right, rather a state of existence that needs to be developed and defended. Freedom is a personal responsibility and as an individual you are accountable. Freedom is not about forcing your values on someone else, nor is it freedom of action as in the situation where you can do whatever you want, even to the detriment of others. Rather freedom is freedom of the mind and freedom of defining your own state of happiness. Freedom, however, demands contribution rather than abuse. Freedom also extends to everyone.

I am proud to say that these basic thoughts became the new tenets of human rights around the world. The now defunct United Nations had adopted the Universal Declaration of Human Rights for individuals in 1947. I remember getting a lot of grief when I argued against that definition of freedom. I had always suggested there was no such thing as a "right" and second, most of the tenets of the UDHR were just platitudes and wishful thinking.

Freedom is also not a universally-defined set of living conditions. China has thrived in the modern world since they embraced certain attitudes toward the treatment of their citizens and extended a free-thinking approach to its citizens while continuing to expect of them the same political and societal obligations. Even now, no one in the USA would characterize China's citizens as free, but they enjoy a standard of living comparable to us, so they feel that their version of freedom is as defendable as ours.

Lastly, during my campaign, I chose to rely on the American public. I didn't hire a campaign manager. I had a staff of six who helped me update the web site and manage my travel schedule but other than that I had no staff and spent virtually no money other than my travel expenses. I had faith that I did not need to strategize by region, plan messaging, spend advertising dollars or hire pollsters to win the election. I put all of my faith in the American people to decide whether they wanted me to be the president. Fortunately the mainstream media could not stop talking about my chances so I got lots of exposure. Prior to me, Donald Trump was "King of the Media", but he faded following my entry into the race. During the 2008 presidential election I saw people get involved with the political process due to the positive and hopeful messages of Barack Obama. The 2016 nomination contests had already been very active and brought many new people into the political realm. I had faith that I could leverage and reignite that spirit, while extending my message to a vast range of Americans.

I genuinely believed that the American public had not lost interest in the political system. I felt that the average American had grown tired of the lack of genuine political discourse, of the negativity and political agendas. Citizens felt that they had no access, no avenue to be heard and that our democracy was too ineffective. They wanted to be involved, but the institutions blocked their access.

One thing that I did realize, however, was that though there might be a lot more interest in the political process, we still had to overcome the public's inhibition to organize themselves. Admittedly I did take a page from the Tea Party movement and asked, on the internet, that my local supporters mobilize election efforts. I was accused of being hypocritical, but I don't think that tells the accurate story. All I did was ask for help.

The local rallies turned out to be a massive part of my presidential bid as "grass-roots" support mobilized the voting community. These folks made the effort to get off the couch and participate in the movement. A few people at the time called it the political revolution of the 21st century, but I disagreed. To me, it was never a revolution, simply an awakening. STAND UP AMERICA simply got people to realize that they were accountable for freedom and democracy. Americans wanted their country, and themselves, to be great again and they were now seeing the time to get active. The previous 50 years of governmental manipulation, lethargy, and anger were being turned around to a more forward and personally-responsible future.

As the voting record shows, I was elected with 55.1% of the popular vote and received the highest number of individual votes ever in the history of presidential elections in the USA. That 55.1% of the popular vote represented over 80,000,000 American citizens. This was a tremendous mandate for me and an overwhelming personal vote of confidence from the American electorate.

Further in the 2016 election, independent candidates won 18% of the available seats in the Congress. The Democrats won the majority position and the Republicans were reduced to less than 25%.

Jumping ahead, in the mid-term election in 2018, the Republicans were virtually eliminated from Congress and the Democrats were reduced to a smattering of candidates. Of the candidates who still represented parties, most were long-standing representatives that had been in their seats for years. However, they campaigned though an allegiance to the new form of government and contribution to the political process, rather than any type of party affiliation.

In 2016, more than 80,000,000 votes was a record and I am proud to say that during my re-election in 2020 I was the first president to ever receive over 100,000,000 votes.

In that 2020 presidential election, the Republican nominee was decimated with only 11.0% of the vote and the Democratic candidate received just 18.8%. This result effectively eliminated the dominance of the party system. I feel very fortunate to have won the 2016 election. I was able to win without compromising my principles. America, by responding to a vision and having trust and faith in a person who was going to run government in a completely different manner, proved itself to me more than I could have dreamed. In hindsight, this is all any American ever really wanted. I look back now, and feel that just about anyone might have won with that concept given how discontented America was at the time. Unlike that random other person however, not only did I have the will to get involved and win, I also was determined to follow through.

CHAPTER 2

THE "NEW FREEDOM INITIATIVE"...A MODERN DEFINITION OF FREEDOM

The foundation of the future America was the "New Freedom Initiative." To me the key to the future was to have the American public in favor of a new direction. I envisioned the "New Freedom Initiative" as redefining exactly what freedom is. For most people at the start of the 21st century, freedom had come to mean the ability to impose your personal thoughts and values onto someone else. Though this is indeed part of what freedom is, it had become too much part of the equation. I had a vision that was more in keeping with the original values of America, that freedom should be about personal contribution, personal being and personal independence rather than imposition of personal values. After the decade-long economic crisis from 2008-2017, many Americans felt that their freedoms had been undercut by economic hardship. I did not agree with this notion, but I had never lost my house or job or experienced economic hardship. I did however come to realize that these Americans were just playing along with societal rhetoric and not really contributing. There had been an expectation amongst this group that, as long as they did the minimum expected, they would receive their version of the American Dream, i.e. home ownership, a car, safe streets and public education. They had come to expect these items by the mere good fortune of being in America. In return, many citizens did nothing for America other than hold a job. America had gotten lazy.

The media, much to my annoyance, instantly dubbed the "New Freedom Initiative" as a personality change for America. I guess in hindsight that is just what it might have been, but the media's initial negativity made everything a lot more difficult, because most Americans did not think they had to change, though of course we ultimately did and the rest of the world wanted us to change too. I have realized over the years that change may not always be required, but change is absolutely necessary if the desire is to maintain leadership. As the rest of the world catches up, a nation has to expand and evolve or fall behind other more progressive nations. In 2017, globalization had the rest of the world gaining ground, while we continued down the same old path of capitalism and self-interest.

Post WWII America grew exponentially more influential in all aspects of modernity. From home appliances, to business methods, to recreational pursuits, America enjoyed a period of prosperity that the world is unlikely to ever see again. Those were very much prosperous and mostly peaceful times. With the "baby boomer" generation, however (those born from 1945-1963), a fierce level of personal selfishness permeated our culture. These children had grown up in a period of peace and their parents had more spending power than ever before. From bikes, to food, to clothes, to education, to recreational items these children were indeed the first "spoiled generation."

Some sociologists have looked back at the late 1960s and seen it as the birth of a humanitarian society from which the boomers espoused the moral purity of peace and love. This of course was the outward appearance, but in my opinion all that free love, excessive drug use, mind expansion philosophy and resistance to societal norms was perhaps the most selfish of actions by any generation in this history of America, if not the world.

Some others have referred to this period as revolutionary, but I disagree with that analysis too. There was no revolution as there was nothing to be revolutionary over. It was simply a rebellious period driven from excessive conservatism by the first generation to grow up in America without want or enemies. Parents and society were caught off guard by the movement. The world went from picket fences and quiet life, to riotous anger in the streets and rejection of existing social norms and values, all in the span of a couple of years. And virtually no one saw it coming.

The hippies' (as they were referred to at the time) goal was to drop out of society and create a new utopia of thought, peace and love. Though each individual aspect is a noble pursuit, how this generation went about these pursuits is beyond reproach and contributed to many of the issues that led the world into the mess of the early 21st century.

Let me be clear. The abandonment of societal norms is about as selfish as you can be. Let's be honest with each other, to reject the values of the previous generation, their economic and social institutions, is the single most selfish act one person can undertake. Self-righteous, it embraces the *certain* knowledge that everything the previous generation has thought is wrong and in many cases *abhorrent* to the younger generation.

This is the first instance of Americans en masse embracing freedom in their own context and rejecting all that has become before them. They saw themselves as smarter, more enlightened and with a better vision than their parents and the establishment. Now, I am not saying that pre-boomer America at the time was an absolute perfect society, but it was following established paths. This is the normal evolution of society, and in fairness, dramatic changes have indeed taken place in the past, but usually the changes that were called for were against despotic and violent rulers. Not against the societal values of a previous generation.

Now, before I go much further, I am willing to accept that government at the time had certainly lost connection with the mass population and deserved some type of resistance. Nonetheless, the US government provided economic stability, consumer products and social institutions which raised the standard of living immeasurably for most American families.

Dropping out of society meant that you were unwilling to contribute to society in terms of offering your value to others. Let's face it, free love and mind expansion do very little to contribute to the development of infrastructure. Wandering aimlessly through society is the ultimate selfishness. It is not love or world peace or revolution, it is simply about being selfish and doing nothing. There are always citizens who contribute nothing to society and those people in today's world are ignored and in my mind that is acceptable. The boomer generation of the 1960s was, however, too large to ignore and their protesting nature made it equally difficult to extricate them from the political and cultural dialogue.

This lack of contribution to society couldn't continue. In the early 1960s we were well down an unstoppable path to prosperity. Boomers profited and American business was the leader in diversifying into global markets. Money was pouring into the USA from all corners of the globe.

However, this infusion of wealth allowed American business to essentially become a trading house for cash and, unfortunately, that contributed to us losing our sense of value. If McDonald's or Coca-Cola reaped more profits from overseas expansion then what incentive was there for further development of their American markets and workforce? American workers, as a result of globalization, sat back and worked 20 hours a week, playing golf and drinking more. Work standards went out the window as hard or smart work was no longer required to achieve profit. The difficult work was farmed out to foreign labor at pennies on the dollar. Let's face it, no one bragged about putting in a hard day's work at the time; it was all about how much money you had accumulated and if you got it easily so much the better.

Investment speculation was another key contributor to the decline of American value. Very few investors looked into the value of a company anymore, nor at who the management was; it was just a quick way to make a few dollars. Now I won't deny that I did a fair amount of this myself as it was just so easy to build wealth by flipping stocks. I bought and sold shares without even really knowing the names of the companies. The average American as well got access to the stock market in the 1980s through the development of mutual funds and this became a big part of just about everyone's retirement package. You could have asked 95% of investors in mutual funds what stocks they held and they would not have known. When you start handing over cash to people without any type of controls or even interest in your portfolios, then why should they care either? Rampant speculation was the result. I recall talking to brokers who would say that they did not want clients who they would have to talk to ten times a week. They charged their fees and had virtually zero stake in whether the individual portfolio went up or down. Fortunately, US stocks were vastly positive throughout this period so most everyone made money. This allowed the system to grow and grow and no one wanted to be the one to put an end to the great gains at the expense of poor and unethical principals. Selfish gains trumped the well-being of others.

I wish the internet had existed at the time. I would have been more than happy to do all my trading myself. I had a reliable firm running my portfolio but I'd still get irked if I got a call from my broker trying to push a stock on me when he couldn't even tell me anything about the company. It wreaked of either one-sided sales, i.e. the broker selling me a stock their firm was vested in, or the broker just trying to make a sale for an additional commission. It was all so lazy and meaningless, yet the financial return was there so it was difficult to pass up. It isn't so hard to see how society got complacent.

Back to the boomer generation. When the 1960s turned out to be just a drug-fueled delusion and the kids realized they needed a couple of dollars and a purpose in order to live their life, they then started entering the work force with purely selfish attitudes. Business started taking on a more profit driven mindset and the desire for more and more profits in a faster time-frame became prevalent. This was fueled by a rampant consumerism that exploded in the 1970s in fashion, style and design that were not as significant in prior decades. A good example of this is the disco movement, whereby outrageous clothes, platform shoes and colourful hairdos were the antithesis of the hippie look, which was drab and dirty. It was like a complete polar opposite of the previous appearance and style. Still it reeked of selfishness and personal uniqueness that usurped conforming to societal norms. Outrageous clothes and hair were the rage but when you look back, it was all quite ridiculous. Drug consumption changed from softer drugs to more designer-drugs like cocaine. Once again, this generation fueled a rampant culture of excess and hedonism that probably hadn't been seen since the days of the Roman Empire. One thing that was retained from the hippie period was the inherent selfishness and the lack of consideration and contribution to America. Everything became "How can I have more of just about everything?" Cars, homes, drugs, clothes, travel.... propped up by the money rolling in from American foreign ownership. This success just continued unabated though the 1980s until it caught up with us.

America had lost its ability to contribute anything of value. Wealth generation became more about financial holdings and real estate than doing something tangible. The blue-collar working class continued to go to work each day but were being left behind in the ridiculous growth of the financial markets and real estate development. What ultimately happened was the collapse of both. This led to America bankrupting itself and losing its place in the international community. In the 1980s there were recessions that forced interest rates up to more than 20%. A lot of people suffered. Even business suffered dramatically as we allowed more and more foreign ownership and access to our markets than we ever had and a lot of our great US companies were now controlled by foreign hands. I am not opposed to this, as it is part of being part of a global economy and US interests own so much of other countries' national businesses that it would be hypocritical to deny them access to our shores. At the time though, I was offended and spoke against handing over ownership to foreign investment, against selling our greatest assets merely to drive stock holder greed.

The 1980s and early 1990s were the "glory days" of the boomer generation, but following that period the economy started to deteriorate rapidly and within 25 years America was on the brink of collapse. Wealth accumulation became the measure of success and business activities certainly reflected this. The bottom-line drove most decisions that were being made and a ridiculous faith in real estate and the market made people oblivious to the going-ons around them. One thing I never did in business or government was take success for granted. Success was earned and not an entitlement.

The 1990s were the culmination of the selfishness of this generation of Americans, by then the boomers had even become known as the "ME" generation. Americans continued to go about their activities as if there were no consequences to their actions.

President Bill Clinton is the premiere example for the prevailing attitude of the times. It is unfathomable that he survived the impeachment process. His ability to separate inappropriate activity from his position as President is a perfect example of what I mean by lack of personal responsibility and lack of consequences. The generation of Americans who supported him forgave him and allowed him to prosper. He became a senior global statesman in the early 21st century. Clinton was the epitome of what was wrong with this generation of Americans and symbolic of the inevitable decline. The fact that he might have been back in the White House as the husband of the President was one of several motivations for getting involved in 2016.

Many people have criticized my views of Bill Clinton and in some instances it is probably justified. At the time I may have appeared hypocritical, as I was equally self-interested in my business and the pursuit of carnal desires. However, I still felt that I contributed to society and deserved some of the excesses and I was single at the time. Plus, I admit that I do tend to judge people of low moral character pretty harshly, especially when they strive for public office. The President should forever be held to higher standards than anyone else in the nation. Yet Clinton demonstrated that not only can inappropriate behavior provide no consequence, it can actually make you more prosperous. This affected the thinking of a whole generation of men. To me, this mindset contributed greatly to the downfall of the family unit at the time. By 2010, the short-lived selfish generation achieved divorce rates higher that 50%.

George W. Bush continued this trend of unaccountable actions following the events of 9/11, having carte blanche to abandon every tenet of democracy and privacy. Bush and his government repurposed the facts, listened to incredulous sources, ignored counter opinions and violated basic American rights so that they could operate without restriction or accountability. To me, Bush should be looked upon as the man who stripped America of its democratic principles.

The ultimate Bush example is the falsified "Weapons of Mass Destruction" information that his government put forth as justification for moving the Afghanistan war into Iraq. The information was collected from an Iraqi informant, who, for large sums of money, told the US government what they wanted to hear. The government then put the information forward to the American people as irrefutable fact to get support for the invasion of Iraq and the ousting of Saddam Hussein.

I had attended a business conference several years before those circumstances in 2002 and the keynote speaker was former President George Herbert Walker Bush. He spent the majority of his time speaking to the fact that they should have "finished the job" after the Kuwait war and removed Hussein while they had the chance. It therefore came as no surprise when George W. Bush invaded Iraq — it was simply the fulfillment of his father's wishes. This was a fundamental violation of democracy; hereditary influence in government was one of the fundamental corner stones that the founding fathers tried to protect against.

So, what is the result of all of this lying? Americans no longer got upset about being lied to, especially over a matter that led us into a significant war in the Middle East that created the Islamic State. I believe this acceptance occurred for two reasons. One, the American public did not like Saddam Hussein and there was lots of ill-will towards anyone in the Middle East due to the lingering anger over 9/11. The rise of Islamic State was simply viewed as an off-shoot of that and not attributed to US activity in the region, though this has now been linked.

The second troubling attitude was the lack of outrage that the government lied to us. By the 21st century, almost every American had developed an innate distrust of government, or, if distrust is too strong a word, an apathetic view of how government operated. Therefore, a lack of desire to listen to them or pay too much attention developed. However, citizens still wanted the US government and military to control the world. We were willing to let the government and military defend our interests without holding them accountable.

One other strange thing at the time was why American culture was so admired outside the US. I could understand the level of modernity and prosperity that our great wealth had delivered for its citizens and I'm sure every country around the world was jealous of the amount of property we held and the conspicuous consumption that the 1990s embraced, all on display by the arrival of new media vehicles like cable TV and the internet. TV shows that celebrated outlandish wealth and music videos that showcased the American way of life set a standard that most Americans did not even have access to. It did make America look attractive, though it was not accurate.

I have been around the world on numerous occasions and the appeal of American pop culture has always shocked me. I understand our nation needs to be entertained, to be catered to and to be excessive. None of these values is in and of itself a bad thing, just the culmination of 30 years of hedonism. Pop culture is mind-numbing and keeps the mass population distracted from more important issues like government, business, well-being and compassion. Now don't get me wrong, Americans have always been generous when called upon for world aide, but when it comes to their own neighbor, not so much.

The new generation of Americans however, in 2016, were demonstrating a growing desire for individuals to become more involved, but it was nowhere at the level of contribution we have today in 2050.

The New Freedom Initiative comprised four basic "cause and effect" aspects. The first was the use of money as a means of establishing a common standard for people. The second was to create a "Spirit of Law and Order" in order to bring back ethics and compassion as key American values. Thirdly, we defined access points in the governmental process so that Americans felt like participants in our country again. And lastly, we instituted the Engaged Democracy model for American government which replaced the representative system.

What emerged was a passion for freedom and democracy such that Americans understood the principles in a 21st century context and could find common ground. Something that the political system had lost sight of due to partisanship.

The first phase of the New Freedom Initiative (NFI) started with the understanding that people tend to judge others in terms of their own station in the world. Some of the Asian cultures didn't spend too much time doing this but in the West we were obsessed with it, and in the 21st century most people's evaluations of others were based on money. People at the time thought racism, religion and personal issues were the core of people's evaluations of others. I knew better than that.

For the first time ever, I will openly reveal that I think money is a much better valuation than someone's personal attributes, like religion or gender. Therefore, I state unequivocally that money is a better common denominator for personal evaluation as it leads to far less prejudice. However, the corollary problem with money at the time as a valuation criterion, is that it provided one individual a quantifiable reason not to respect the value of another's human life and it minimizes the importance of morality involved in the attainment of money.

In the early 21st century, the simple fact that you had money gave the possessor inequitable power and influence. Business and moral ethics went out the window as companies and people strived to have more money than the person next door. As a result, the value of many people's contribution to society went to zero, yet their personal influence sky-rocketed due to their wealth. Not to cast aspersions, but corrupt lawyers and unethical CEOs made America a very disillusioned nation by not creating an equitable playing field. Poor corporate and social behavior, such as down-sizing, became the norm. Profits trumped people in almost every case.

The wealthy went about their money-making ventures with impunity, for who was affected by their bad actions and money-collecting ways? If people were trampled or killed along the way then so be it. If people lost all their possessions then so be it.

If foreign nationalists were exploited then so be it. If the earth was polluted and destroyed, that was just a cost of business. Any action in pursuit of making money was implemented and tolerated. Unfortunately, this method of operation spread to a lot of other emerging capitalist regions and the same model occurred. In worst case scenarios, dictators sucked money out of the business and political world while killing their own people. Even in developed areas such as Ireland, Portugal, Iceland, France, Brazil and Greece, the results of this mode of operation ultimately led to collapses.

Changing mindsets was what the NFI strived to accomplish. In 2017, wealthy American citizens felt that they could operate as they wished without threat of prosecution or any tangible consequences. Since the 1960s, the population at large had become unapologetic for its actions, and anything detrimental was automatically someone else's fault. Ultimately two things happened: the first was that a system of reward for failure was created. In this system, you could sue people for wrong-doing even though nothing was done wrong and you could receive recognition from being notorious or dishonest. The reality was that being dishonest or unethical quite often paid better than trying to do things the right way. The second was that people lost their sense of initiative. Too many people simply blamed their ill-fortune or bad circumstances on someone else. The government of course being the primary scapegoat. President Obama was blamed throughout his term for not creating enough jobs for ordinary people. Or, on the other hand, that he tried to create more social programs. Either way you looked at it, there was an universal mindset that individuals did not have to be responsible for themselves as in the previous era. The American Dream of working hard to achieve success was gone. America's "lazy success" at the end of the 20th century had infiltrated every aspect of American life and made us a very soft country.

The "New Freedom Initiative" set out to redefine people's worth and perceived value based on their level of contribution to society. The goal was to have those who contributed the most receive the highest level of rewards. In the 1960s JFK had the famous adage "Ask not what your country can do for you, but what you can for your country." That American spirit is one that I have leveraged numerous times. That overachieving mindset was what made America great in the early years, during the Industrial Revolution and the mid-20th century. I had no doubt that recapturing this spirit and was clearly what was required in 2017. The NFI was a reminder of what America is.

The first tangible act was to impose more severe punishment for criminal acts and unethical business practices. The number one problem in the 21st century was that anyone with money could pretty much do whatever they wanted without consequence. This changed virtually overnight with the institution of the "Spirit of Law" Act. It was a ground-breaking restatement of general principles of law and order that had eroded over the years. Within that "Spirit of Law" Act, the key tenet was that the intent of any federal legislation became legally binding. I will discuss the now ubiquitous "Spirit of Law" Act in Chapter 3.

Secondly, lawyers' compensation models were dramatically changed and the entirety of the legal process was shortened. Detailed explanation will be in Chapter 6.

Thirdly, the federal level of police work, i.e. the FBI and CIA, were repurposed to defend private citizens' interests rather than to investigate them. State policy for municipal police forces focused more on detecting illegal activity, solving crimes and subsequently persecuting the charged. The days of simply reacting to violent crimes, which had been the traditional role of policing, was reduced in relation to the amount of time that was expended against it.

Law and order in the streets was still the number one priority, but other areas were enhanced, such as the ability to seek out and persecute private-sector crime. For example, a police department's ability to be involved in white collar crime was negligible up until the "Spirit of Law" Act, but those powers were extended dramatically within the principles of the NFI. Regulation was also strengthened to facilitate these formal roles.

The Securities and Exchange Commission (SEC) under the oversight of Congress in the early days of my Presidency became a zealous watchdog for domestic and international companies doing business within the USA. The bottom-line was that if you were going to do business in the USA, you had to adopt an ethical and honest approach to your operations, financing and consumers. Businesses were expected to operate with the spirit of these regulations, policies and laws rather than just offer a window-dressing effort at adhering to them. Business had resisted any type of governmental oversight, which they considered intrusive. It was obvious in 2008 that they had created the current fiscal nightmare yet they were still unwilling to allow outside regulation. Of course, American citizens and the international business community had such little faith in the US business sector, and as profits started to drop it became clear that Wall Street needed to adhere to a spirit of law and improved operations just to survive. They couldn't do it themselves.

I fully expected to hand the SEC over to the financial sector for self-regulation when they had proved their ability to see that good regulation and honest operation would deliver substantive profits. This proved to be the case and to this day the SEC is the gold standard of all government agencies. For example, when the department of biotechnology began in 2018, they put a similar management structure into place as well as developed a series of principles that very much reflected those implemented by the SEC.

The third provision of the NFI was to restore people's faith in the abilities of the federal government and the democratic principles that the USA was founded upon. As part of an internet movement to collect real feedback, I invited all opinions. For the first time in the history of the USA there was a Department of American Communications, which was 100% dedicated to talking to and discussing issues with American citizens. I will readily admit that the motivation was not necessarily to listen to anyone's particular opinion, but rather to restore faith in American democracy and the office of the presidency. Prior to my entering the race for president, I held a strong belief that the presidency was an undemocratic position. America voted for the chosen party representative every four years and were ignored the rest of the time. I do not consider ticking a ballot every four years as democracy. Citizens have to have greater influence than that.

To me, the presidency was a powerful symbol of freedom and the democratic process for the rest of the world. A position of intelligence, might, and most of all a defender of the Constitution and the multitude of freedoms that the USA was trying to promote in the world. The office of the presidency should be the number one proponent and defender of these same liberties.

The oath of office makes the president's role extremely clear:

> *"I do solemnly swear that I will faithfully execute the Office of President of the United States, and will to the best of my ability, preserve, protect and defend the Constitution of the United States."*

Over the previous 40 to 50 years this oath has essentially been abandoned. By 2017, the Presidency had devolved into being merely a position for the top party representative. This person ultimately is beholden to the parties themselves and the Constitution has been forsaken. Therefore, I made the assertion that the President did not represent America.

The democratic ideals and principles of the US had been completely usurped.

The goal of the Dept. of American Communications was to give the typical American the sense that someone was listening and that each individual should take the opportunity to be part of the democratic process. The representative democracy was useless.

By having a direct line of communication to staffers in the President's office, people started to feel that they had a stake in their government. They started to care more about their country and feel that it was worth investing some of their personal time and energy into its future. This is all America ever really needs from its citizens.

CHAPTER 3

THE BIRTH OF THE NEW MODEL OF GOVERNMENT "ENGAGED DEMOCRACY"

The fourth portion, and most important, of the "New Freedom Initiative" was the redefinition of freedom and a new democratic model which suited the modern era. To be honest, these were essentially self-defined by the American people rather than delivered by my government. My hope though was to very much guide the discussion and the political agenda so that as a nation we could arrive at a modern definition of each, such that we had commonly established principles to move forward.

The greatest American cultural obstacle I had to overcome upon becoming President was the bias people held toward the notion of contribution. We needed to redefine freedom and what it meant and represented. It was this poor definition of freedom, coupled with a flawed political system that held Barack Obama back from achieving anything during his term in office. Ultimately, he started to do get things done when he bowed to the politics of the party system at the time. And sadly, what he achieved was far removed from what he had hoped for and promised during his first election. Following the debt-ceiling fiasco in mid-2011 where Obama had to acquiesce to Republican authority and then implement the infamous Super Committee debacle, all hope was gone that Obama would be able to make a difference. He was only able to win again in 2012 due to the ineptitude of the Republicans, but his final four years were ineffective as well.

Like Obama, I probably would have succumbed to the same obstacles if I had not chosen to attack these two cultural areas (freedom and democracy) directly.

The most misguided thought that became embedded in the American psyche was that concern for people or elements of society was equal to socialism or communism.

By 2009, any proponent of compassionate governmental policy was called a socialist who was striving to undermine the entirety of the USA. That may sound melodramatic but phrases like that were actually used at the time by American citizens. I remember when President Obama was trying to implement the universal health insurance program, so that more American citizens would have access to health care. Yet this system, which cared about the general health of all citizens, was considered akin to Nazism by some people. Even to this day that still strikes me as the most absurd type of rhetoric, and I privately argued at the time that it should be akin to hate speech. To utilize Nazi imagery in an American political debate is simply immoral on any level.

Senator Bernie Sanders (the Democratic candidate who lost to Hillary Clinton in 2016) faced the same type of response during his campaign. Sanders was a self-characterized socialist and his policies of income equality, health care subsidies and corporate regulation reflected his philosophy. However, he certainly did not deserve the demeaning characterizations that were tossed in his direction. There is nothing wrong with espousing a philosophy that entitles the majority of citizens to receive adequate education and health care. He was simply fighting for a fairer America. Being as I was at the top of the income ladder, I was aware of the numerous benefits available to those in my income level. Let's face it, I would never have been encouraged to run for president were I not wealthy. That Sanders got significant support early in the 2016 primary races was encouraging. He was not going to defeat Hillary Clinton for the Democratic nomination, but he did draw genuine attention to his campaign. I recognized this swing in political motivation, and received much of his support as my campaign gained momentum.

I digress. The Republican Party and the Tea Party Movement were mostly to blame for the vile rhetoric and as early as 1980 they had come to the point where political expediency was their paramount goal. Rhetoric could be founded upon any truth or untruth and could even be what many folks would consider slanderous. The shocking thing about this situation is that so many American citizens accepted this rhetoric and supported it. I can understand that there was disillusion in the US at the time due to the 2008 economic collapse, but to sink to such lows should have been offensive to more people. This is why I argued so strongly that a new definition of freedom was needed. As a nation we had sunk too far in our willingness to allow anyone to do or say whatever they chose in the political arena.

Just about every election, regardless of level of government, of the late 20th century and early 21st century was essentially run as an attack campaign against their opponent, and the Republican Party in particular became a machine to spew political propaganda as well as to be the virulent voice of hypocrisy and frivolous opinion. No member of the Republican Party seemed to have any remorse for slandering innocent people nor did they object to embracing whatever position seemed to impose the greatest hurt on the Democratic opposition. This was especially evident whenever the Obama administration attempted any type of humanitarian effort.

Donald Trump, who successfully ran for the Republican party nomination in 2016, got to the point where he ran a right-wing campaign based almost exclusively on racism, vitriol and bullying.

As mentioned, the Republicans had made the concept of human compassion symbiotic with weakness and socialism as a way to stem government spending and control the political agenda. The entire concept of government intervention through social programs was frowned upon. They promulgated a free market and complete governmental non-intervention. They attempted to repeal taxes, increase military spending and force each person to fend for themselves. Of course, their underlying motivation was wealth generation and economic control for America's elite rather than any overall American improvement.

I would never have won the election in 2016 if the Republicans had not been so divisive and offensive to so many Americans.

It took many concerted efforts on my part to get the message to sink in that considering the outcome of other American citizens was not "un-American." From the birth of America, the basic standard was considered to be fairness and equal access to services and institutions without punitive persecution. The primary issue that I set out to disseminate to the middle class was that they did not in fact have equal access to government nor were they being treated fairly by previous administrations. This was most true in the case of their recent presidents as well as by the manner in which Congress and government in general conducted itself. Most Americans, it is fair to say, did not even have access to the institutions of government. The representative democratic system had abandoned them.

Through my election campaign and my first months in office, Americans came to realize that they would indeed have a voice and a role in the process.

What would become known as the "Engaged Democracy" model of democratic government began with a desire to consult with a broad range of American citizens, which we did through the Dept. of American Communications. We would consult with the fringe element on every issue, then with the experts and then the interested voters. Americans came to see that it was not only the financial and political interests that had a say.

This frustration and disengagement was now countered with a profound interest in the issues of the day and the desire to see resolutions that benefited the greater good of America, rather than just the special interests and the wealthy. At no time did citizens feel that they were losing their individual freedom; most Americans felt that they were gaining it back. Soon, most Americans saw the betterment of the majority, along with whatever individual benefit they hoped for. It is fair to say that most people want to see their overall condition improve, but not at the direct expense of their neighbors. I have always believed this. Polls showed, that when involved in the process, that the great majority of voters would vote for the direction that took into consideration the widest influence for their families and friends over their individual best interest. When it came to issues of health and well-being, taxes were even considered beneficial for the stability and the best interest of America as a country.

The secret to my success as President, was understanding that if you gave the moderate Americans access to government, then the fringe influence and party interests would be minimized. These results hearkened back to an era when Americans put America ahead of their personal interests. When signs of this feeling became evident, I knew we were on the right track. These attitudinal changes were led primarily by the younger generation who had not grown up in such a selfish manner as their parents and seemed to have a broader view than the one provided from their own front porch.

The ability for anyone to register as an interested party on any piece of policy development legislation was a brand new concept in 2017 and essentially signalled the beginning of the end for representative democratic government.

"Engaged Democracy", where all interested parties and stake-holders are involved from start to finish of the legislative process became the preferred model.

The representative portion of government, of course, still exists today, but elected officials serve as the managers of the public process, and their legislative and power-yielding days are long gone. From an early age it had always bothered me that an elected official was supposed to represent my interests. I have always felt that no single person can have well-developed opinions on every single issue and I would not expect even myself to have expert knowledge on every issue. Plus, as a representative, you were supposed to be the voice of your constituents, even though they likely know as much, if not more, on any given issue than you do. Therefore, almost by definition, representative democracy could not work as it is unreasonable to expect that one person can represent all of their constituents on every issue. Take myself for instance. I know virtually nothing about mining or fisheries. Why, then, would I lead policy in either of these areas? However, the representative system at the time demanded it, even from the President. In 2016 none of the best and brightest of American society was willing to place themselves into the political process. Political life was just too public, inefficient and frustrating for anyone who actually considered themselves talented. Testament to this was the talent pool who put themselves forward to be president in 2016.

By the 1970s, partisan party politics had made representative democracy essentially meaningless as well. Party members, once elected, were expected to vote in terms of the party position rather than of the wants of their constituents.

The role of lobbyists and cash influence had made "pure" politics, those based on morals or ethics, completely null and void. Citizens who got involved were those who were the most passionate about their specific cause. They would show up for rallies, write letters, make donations to organizations and basically do whatever it took to force their agenda. This approach, though completely adequate and even admirable, had gotten a disproportionate amount of attention from the media, moneyed interests and subsequently politicians. The moderate portion of America, those who were not quite as passionate or perhaps willing to find a compromise, were pushed aside. Therefore the fringe interests got preferential treatment.

Finally, and this was a big issue in 2016, there was little accountability for anyone in office. They did not respond to the electorate other than trying to win the next election, which is ultimately what each member of the House of Representatives and the Senate spent the most of their time doing. Once elected, it was pretty tough to be unseated due to the power of the parties, the gerrymandering of ridings and the influence of lobbyist cash.

As a result, the best course of action to getting re-elected came down to doing as little as possible. Advancement followed anyone who was successful, but success had to be continuous. Failures were so exacerbated by your opposition that retaining your seat was next to impossible. The most important issue though for political advancement was loyalty to the party. If an individual had any political aspiration at all, it was best to follow the party line rather than charting your own course.

In 2011, I made the case in a controversial speech that America was no longer a democratic country. As a corollary, most citizens did not feel as if they had much of a say and the majority of citizens felt that they certainly did not have any influence over government policy or direction. Involvement in politics on any issue of the day was rarely desired and the gap between those holding power, and those who did not, was so wide that it struck to the fundamentals of what being an American was even about. To most people it simply meant freedom to make money in whatever way possible.

But I believed our greatness was going to be regained through contribution and communication. With the advent of the social networks that we developed, we were always able to listen to any citizen who had an opinion. This served a great many purposes on the heels of the election. The most important was not just in terms of developing an appropriate direction for public policy but also developing legislation that actually worked and delivered objectives. This might sound like common sense but it certainly was not the way it worked when my government arrived in January of 2017. At the time, the process to develop legislation and policy was ineffective, confusing, inaccessible and downright self-serving.

In the old days, most legislation was discussed and developed behind closed doors. We changed all that with the "Engaged Democracy" model.

In our approach, as soon as the legislation committee was undergoing its initial discussions, citizens were invited to provide stories of cause and effect, or hoped-for outcomes, suggestions of policies, political views, whatever they felt appropriate, like the letters to the editors section of a local newspaper. Government bureaucrats were assigned to maintain, monitor and collect more feedback as required. This use of government bureaucracy, to collect feedback from citizens, was considered astounding in 2017; this was the first time bureaucrats would call people for clarification and or more information on their comments. As an aside, elected officials started touting the number of times they talked to constituents and Americans in their election ads as of 2018. Now that to me was a great campaign to run on. I deserve to be in Congress because I talk to and listen to Americans. What a concept.

As part of the original "3POI-P" process (to be covered in Chapter 4), each committee established a timeline that had to be adhered to for deliverables. For most policy-development platforms three months was the longest period available to deliver a first draft and then within 45 days the final draft had to be delivered. It was followed by a ten-day voting period. The whole process rarely took more than six months. In fact, after the first couple of years simple policy documents were done in less than two months. Other basic actions, such as amendments, could have been done in less than a week, but we did not want to get in the habit of skipping due diligence or providing Americans the opportunity to get involved. The point was not to be fast, but rather inclusive and democratic.

The final stage, once the final draft was completed, was direct voting for the legislation in question by the interested Americans who had a stake in the result. We would then be bound by the result of the voting. This was a contentious issue at the time and considered by some to be undemocratic as the entirety of the American voting pool was not represented in the voting process. Putting motions through the normal representative Congressional voting procedures, one could at least make the argument that all Americans were represented and that democracy was more fulfilled.

To the critics of this voting process, I countered with two distinct views that represented not only an American democratic history lesson but also represented a version of American government that was needed for the 21st century, rather than a system that was 300 years old.

My fundamental belief was that every single American need not have to be represented for a bill to become a law. I think this is self-evident in the concept of majority rules. It is pretty safe to say that 100% participation has never been an aspiration of the democratic process in any part of the world. It follows that if you can get a majority from the most interested citizens, then that should be more than sufficient to enact legislation. Let's face it, even back when America was being born, not every American citizen wanted to part from England. The majority did, and it turned out to be the right thing to do.

It is still not unreasonable to conclude that many of the issues of the world were and still are overly complex. On the opposite end, many of the issues of the world are overly mundane. Neither aspect of governmental operation should expect that most American citizens would have an interest, let alone a say, in the appropriate course of action or legislation. For example, in the areas of taxation, though the citizenry has a general interest in what perhaps the taxation rates are, none of them likely have that same interest in the working and development of the legislation that is to be enacted. Those who do care, however, have every right to be involved and should lead the thinking for the legislation.

Through my second argument, in keeping with my driving premise of the "NFI", the intention of the founding fathers from 225 years prior was able to be adhered to. However, the institutions that have evolved over that same period were no longer conducive to democratic fulfilment and were incapable of addressing the issues of the time. Further, Congress in 2016 was certainly not the mechanism required to move forward. It was time to change how the operations of government were done while maintaining the spirit of freedom and democracy.

As important as the "NFI" turned out to be in terms of redefining freedom and democracy, the implementation and reinforcement was delivered through the development of the concept of the "Spirit of Law." It might seem odd in 2050 that the "Spirit of Law" did not exist just 35 years ago. The "Spirit of Law" became the foundation of guidance for modern society simply by giving the intent of legislation equal footing in law with the terms and conditions as they were written. Today, most of our actions are defined by intent rather that the outcome. With the "Spirit of Law" we needed to collect as much feedback as possible on the "spirit" of our policy and legislation. Afterwards, we would have an easier time framing the legislation itself.

For example, in early 2017, we initially tried to enact a simplistic type of "Spirit of Law" for taxation: "Every citizen and corporation is obligated to contribute a fair share of income on an annual basis." This met with very little favourable feedback and it was considered too general and lacking in terms of more tangible clauses. It was felt that a "Spirit of Law" of this nature would have no meaningful impact. It was also agreed that if the intention of the "Spirit of Law" was to carry legal ramifications as much as the specific legislation then it needed stronger language.

Our second attempt read as follows: "With full recognition that the United States of America's government requires operating capital in order to carry out domestic and international obligations and to contribute to the overall improvement of America's well-being, it is recognized that every American citizen and corporation is, by law, required to submit no less than an absolute minimum of 7.5% of their personal annual income as federal tax. Income taxes will be incurred as an increasing percentage of income per the stipulated guidelines as outlined in the Taxation Codes."

I personally expected that there would be outrage; we were essentially institutionalizing paying taxes. But I was pleasantly surprised. Other than a few small specific groups of American society and the challenges which argued that legislating taxation was unconstitutional, most "middle class" people realized that taxation is simply a fact of American life. I expected to receive tremendous backlash from the special interests, and I did. However, the fact that we had invited the moderates into the discussion mitigated the special interests' influence. They were out-numbered by millions, which made their concerns seem self-serving, inequitable and unjust. This is exactly what I had hoped might happen, but to see the media turn against the lobbyists and the wealthy was extremely satisfying.

Per the argument itself about paying taxes, the infusion of moderates into the discussion proved to be the stabilizing and collaborative force I expected. To the average citizen, it is no shock that taxes are collected by governments everywhere and people know that these taxes are utilized to provide infrastructure, military operations, educational facilities and other services and programs too many to number. Also, the amounts stipulated in the "Spirit of Law" proviso were actually less than what most people were already paying, so it was palatable. Plus, the situation whereby wealthy citizens and corporations were now required, by law, to pay a designated minimum amount of tax was acceptable because people were upset with the high-income earners and the corporations that found their way around paying their fair share of taxes due to legislative loopholes.

The primary concept that Americans embraced was that corporations were now legally obligated to contribute a minimum level as taxation and also legally obligated to contribute to the betterment of the American public as this was the "Spirit of Law." American companies could remain 100% profit-oriented, but would have to do it with a slightly adjusted attitude. The big difference with the "Spirit of Law" provision, was that companies could no longer find loopholes in taxation legislation. The action would undermine the "Spirit of Law" and was thereby considered criminal activity. Voters who went through the "Engaged Democracy" process (as it existed in 2017) agreed 73% with this "Spirit of Law" as written. We also achieved 60% of eligible voter response for this important issue. We made the case that corporations should accept the will of the people and go along with this new proposal rather than fighting it in the courts. Many companies however took the government to court and 2018 was a long year as a result. In the court of public opinion though, these court actions were considered inappropriate, "un-American." In the new era of "Engaged Democracy," citizens realized that they had the power and that individuals and companies that did not comply with the democratic results were being treasonous. Now in all fairness access to the courts and challenging government is part of the freedom that we were trying to protect, but it does represent though just how strongly individuals were coming to realize that their collective will had more influence than any individual effort.

The level of citizen commitment to the new taxation legislation and the simple fact that so many people had been involved in the voting and had an interest in the taxation turned out to be a changing point in American voter psychology. National retailers who had argued the loudest against the legislation suffered the most. Retailers that had agreed with the legislation or said nothing reaped immediate benefits. Corporations quickly realized that an inspired consumer base had taken back the power in the USA. The days of corporate greed and profiteering at the expense of everyday Americans were over and the old adage of "consumer power" had returned. The era of "Constructive Capitalism" was just around the corner. (See Chapter 5).

Elected members in the House of Representatives had to do some rethinking of their priorities as well following the by-elections in 2018. Many who had aligned themselves with the corporations were voted out of their positions. The electorate clearly indicated that their representatives were required to represent their interests. They were also obligated to manage the "Engaged Democracy" process in a fair and unbiased manner. In an unanticipated event, members of the House and Senate actually started refusing corporate contributions to their campaigns for fear of being labeled as supportive of that company.

A great example is Brookstone Corp. Brookstone took tremendous heat by being seen as "un-American" for resisting the new legislation and became the target of an on-line movement to boycott their goods to the point where their CEO had to publicly apologize to the American people. During the broadcast, as part of his apology, he resigned. It was a proud moment for me. Having been so alienated by government and the system and corporations just a few years prior, it was a tremendous pleasure to watch Americans set the agenda again.

Perhaps I was being unfair to the wealthy and the corporations and holding them to unreasonable standards and on a few occasions perhaps even holding the boardroom hostage. But, it was the right thing to do and corporations became so much more in tune with consumers and started taking a much more practical and humane methodology that had an immediate effect on the world. As mentioned in Chapter 1, companies became more interested in making a positive difference wherever they did business and as a result corporate funds were channeled in a much more positive and beneficial area of society. This of course brought immediate improvements to America, snowballing as companies, upon seeing the impact of their efforts on society at large raced to do more and more to help.

The nice thing about consumers as well is that they do understand what is possible and what is not. Most people realized that environmental change, for example, would not happen overnight and no one expected this of any corporation. They did expect corporations to improve in this area and to develop products that were consistent with ecological efforts. Companies that hired scientists over lawyers started making more and more profit as their products became more and more valuable.

As a result, and as an example of more equitable distribution of wealth, scientists and engineers saw their salaries go up dramatically and many even started their own companies. The sciences now offer some of the highest paying careers in the US of A. As a result, America once again has become a world leader in the sciences, which attracted more people into the scientific community.

Not surprisingly, once corporations understood the real benefit of being a corporate citizen their profits started to increase as well despite them actually paying a fair share of taxes. This is one of the greatest achievements of my presidency was to make corporate leaders finally understand that investing in America would help their bottom line. In return, a highly educated, wealthy and healthy workforce improved quality, efficiency and innovation. It is still booming, as we know, and American corporate success today rivals the successes of the early 20th century. And more people have benefited.

One big taxation change was to lower the rate on foreign income of individuals and corporations. We did this as simply as possible and chose a flat rate. We wanted a lot of the overseas funds, those sitting in foreign banks, returned to America. As of 2016, corporate tax rates were so high on overseas income that most companies would keep those funds overseas as part of international operations. The irony of this was though the corporation was an American one, few of those revenues from overseas operations ever returned to America so there was no benefit other than to the executives and the shareholders of the corporations, a horrendous waste of resources to the entire government.

In 2018, we put in a flat tax of 13.65% on revenues returned to the USA. This amount was reduced to 10% if all or a portion of those funds were allocated directly to employees in the USA. The influx of capital to the USA during this period essentially created a new level of wealth in America and de facto ended a six-year financial crisis. The mortgage crisis ended, auto sales increased dramatically, people paid off their credit cards and started saving for their kid's education.

The funds the government collected from the overseas revenue was staggering. The amounts returning were in the trillions of dollars so therefore the tax revenue was also substantial. A great number of companies of course took advantage of the one-time opportunity to share the funds with their employees and bonus checks were being sent out regularly. As a result, spending and consumption sky-rocketed domestically. The income taxes and sales taxes that the government received amounted to $2.4 trillion and allowed us to lower our national debt to below one trillion dollars for the first time in twenty years.

In response to the improved economic health of our economy and budget we were able to not only improve our overall standard of operations and programs and services, but we and the States were also able to pass tax savings onto the American people. The lowering of gas taxes led to gas prices dropping below $2 a gallon. We were also able to target certain industries that might be struggling for tax relief. But, being rather ingenious with our planning, we passed the tax relief onto the consumers rather than trying to offer initiatives to the businesses themselves. An example? Airlines were able to offer flights without sales taxes. This resulted in a tremendous upswing for air travel without any lost revenue to the airlines. Couple this legislation with the new

"Spirit of Law" legality and airlines were not able to increase prices either to offset the lowering costs. As a result the airline industry boomed and after two years we were able to reinstate sales tax on ticket purchases, but we did so at a lower rate. The government was now able to plan the future of America. This was at the time when the USA purchased a big portion of Eastern Canada in 2022 (see Chapter 7), the first geographic expansion of the USA in over a hundred years.

We also looked to many new areas of taxation rather than relying on personal and corporate tax.

For example, consumption taxes. The intent was not to target specific areas that had broad-based users, but rather aspects of society that were purely voluntary. Areas such as alcohol and cigarette consumption, ammunition purchase or luxury items. People had the choice. We made it clear that there would be no more hidden taxes and, for example, the price of a cigarette package was disclosed as $4 and the tax was $6. This was really no more than the average packet of cigarettes cost than before but, as a result, consumption of tobacco products decreased as people chose not to pay the tax. However, on luxury items where prices varied, the sales tax was increased to 20% which proved not to be a deterrent as products continued to fly off the shelves, especially since disposable income had increased so much for individual consumers.

We knew that these targeted consumers had no problem paying for luxury items and products like high-end vodkas and hand bags had proven that price was never going to be a deterrent when image was concerned.

The coup de gras in regard to consumption taxes were luxury taxes imposed on vehicles $100,000 and over. These high-end cars were taxed at 50% of their value and sales did not diminish. In fact, the higher end vehicles like Bentleys and Lamborghinis saw sales increase as there was a increase to the perceived exclusivity.

Another tax avenue was the controversial era of marijuana legalization, which began in 2021, sourced new, sales-related income.

We could never have done this without the "Engaged Democracy" process. How to control drug usage in America was a constant challenge in the early 20th century, ranging from outright "War on Drugs" to states implementing their own laws for sales. We made it work by asking Americans to decide the law for themselves. We resolved issues about who could use marijuana, where it could be grown, who could sell it, how it would be taxed and other than a few small hiccups, it was the first time that the process proved how effective and broad it could be. "Engaged Democracy" has been working great ever since.

The fact that marijuana legalization created a whole new economic sector in a period of decline and the federal and state taxes were astronomical, that action alone has proved to be one of the most successful legislative actions of the 21st century.

One of the fundamental tenets of past taxation legislation was that sales taxes had to be uniform. Once we overcame this flawed thinking, sales taxes could vary by the product in question as well as the cost of the product. This enabled the government to optimize revenue while also optimizing the opportunity to have those who purchase the most, pay higher amounts due to their higher disposable income. The wealthier part of American society argued that this was discriminatory, but as we had built in the fact that you did not have to purchase the goods in question and that same good would also incur the same tax level to any buyer, that group did not have a legal issue on which to stand. Once again, personal freedom is maintained. These concepts seem completely logical by today's standards, but the boomer generation in the 2000s had a sense of selfish entitlement whereby they thought everything was for their benefit. We did get beaten back in one area however. We specifically targeted homes in specific zip code areas and attempted to implement a federal home transfer tax of 15%. We thought this might be appropriate, as it was a discretionary purchase against wealthier individuals. This time we had clearly violated the spirit of democracy and it became quite clear that trying to implement taxation based on the part of America where you lived was, quite simply, wrong. The defining principle of the "Engaged Democracy" model is that as a government, you cannot ignore the will of the people.

Personally, throughout the whole taxation discussions I always felt that as a wealthier individual I should pay a fair portion of my income but not be excessively taxed. That felt like punishment for being successful. With the attempt to impose taxes geographically I very much crossed the line. We retracted that bill immediately.

This situation, though, showed the power of the true democratic community that we now found ourselves in. Anyone who was interested in the results of any type of policy or legislation could go on-line and contribute their thoughts and feelings to the process. It became pretty clear when policy was not reflecting the will of the American people and Congress would rewrite and modify the direction or the intent and the actual language itself. It is a particularly effective process. The main thing about democracy is that the government realizes that it is merely the voice of the people. It has no authority beyond that to rule.

One final area that I would like to touch on was the decision we reached to tax religious organizations at a flat rate of 2.5%. We felt that, at a minimum, religions should be contributing their fair share to taxes as well within the "Spirit of Law." I personally did not see how paying taxes was in any way shape or form a violation of religious freedom as the taxation would be applied equally to all denominations and all sizes of churches. The intent was not to impose regulation over any religious organization and this is why we attached a much lower amount of taxation to these groups. Personal income tax deductions of individuals were not affected by this legislation.

I expected a battle over this and it did indeed turn out to be the toughest one of my presidency. The criticism was relentless and the foundations of most arguments were based in faith, so there were really few rational responses I could muster.

There were protests of thousands on the steps of the White House and on the national mall and I was inundated by responses from religious leaders not only in the USA but around the world. The Pope weighed in and I got several calls from King William regarding the issue in relation to the Anglican Church.

Of course, the issue was separating of church and state and freedom of religion. I also viewed it as an element of hypocrisy and greed from groups that relied on contributions from their congregation to run their operations. Let's face it, you can utilize semantics however you want but the concept of a tithe as a gift to the church and God is no different than a gift to the USA just under the guise of a tax. The main difference philosophically is that you can claim that one is voluntarily while the other is forced.

As we had stated in our "Spirit of Law" the goal was simply to have American people and organizations contribute a fair share to the overall betterment of the country. Religious groups were part of America and therefore should not be exempt from contributing. Keep in mind that many members of religious movements viewed themselves as significant contributors to societal interests and were not necessarily interested in avoiding the tax. Also, many members of the congregation thought that by giving taxes they might more effectively contribute beyond the simple realm of their church. Christian religions value sacrifice and brotherly acceptance, which worked to soften some of the resentment that the government was working its way into the operation of their religious institutions.

It took a long time for me and the government to start to make in-roads in this area. As everyone knows, I was baptized a Roman Catholic but did not maintain the formalized portion of my upbringing. However, I certainly embraced the Christian values of fellowship, compassion and love. These are the aspects of religions that I wanted to see become more predominant in society.

The bottom-line however, was that through the "Engaged Democracy" and "3POI-P" methodology, the vast majority of Americans had indicated they would like to see religious groups paying taxes. Therefore, this was my mandate as President. Not to lead the initiative or acquiesce to special interests, but rather to take direction from American citizens and make their will the law of the land.

This as we know now in 2050 is the role of every elected member of Congress.

CHAPTER 4

THE "3POI-P" APPROACH... ABORTION AND IMMIGRATION EXAMPLES

To most people, "Engaged Democracy" will be my legacy. When I get questioned, it's the thing most people want to know: how was I able to advance us out of a seemingly hopeless situation? What's my approach to such challenges?

Firstly, I have found that most complex issues are really just made-up political situations and have become complicated due to the inability of people in positions of authority to identify the problem in the first place, identify the correct objective or even worse they create circumstances that serve their own agenda. Eliminate these three areas for confusion and most issues are not nearly as complicated as one would think. The mindset to start with is that you are not actually trying to solve problems. The reality is that the world is extremely fluid and all one can do is continue to move the process back and forth such that progress is being made and people spend more time focused on progress rather than fighting with each other. One further needs to recognize that most issues involve a moral issue and that people's individual lives will be affected, therefore they do have a stake in the outcome.

The secret is to not establish a goal that incurs dramatic sweeping change as the infrastructure is rarely in place to deal with change of that nature. Rather, one needs to bring all parties to a common place. This way everyone involved knows the expected result, but how to get there is fluid. The other thing, is to include as many interested people as possible. Large support delivers movement. The final secret is to understand that correction will be required due to public opposition. I tend to look at cultural change as a pendulum. There will always be a series of swings in thinking and programs. The issues will be debated exhaustively over time and the programs refined, such that an equilibrium will be reached whereby many people are satisfied and the issue can be considered less important. It will never be perfect or without exceptions, but the multitude will have concurred that they are in the right place. The final piece of the puzzle is to know, with all certainty, that not everyone will be satisfied.

On the challenges of "advancement," whether in business, politics, international or personal relations, my primary methodology has always been what is now referred to as the "3POI-P" process. People of Interest, Politics of Interest and Positions of Interest. 3POI-P is taught in universities around the world and it the accepted way to collect information and address problems. I personally have never used the phrase, but for my purposes here I will. I look at the entire 3POI-Process as a system whereby the parties involved each have to exert energy, go through ups and downs yet ultimately move the entire system to a new place. If one person or group exerts too much force, or opposing sides exert equivalent force at the same time, neither side advances other than in moments when the other party shows weakness. This is never effective.

At polar ends of any social issue are the extreme people, politics or positions whereby one party or group wants everything and the other group nothing. Under this scenario, the issue can indeed be resolved by force, but only one side achieves advancement.

In the middle balanced position, each party achieves fifty percent of its goals, which creates equilibrium. The equilibrium however should never remain in the middle as this would be a stagnant position. In reality, an equilibrium position is by nature impossible to maintain due to fluctuating conditions.

The ideal process becomes a give and take built on the effort of each party which leads to all parties having ups and downs but in an environment where each stake-holder receives some benefit. In 3POI-P, maximum momentum is achieved when competing interests contribute to the maximum of their ability and at the right point.

The other primary aspect of 3POI-P is the invitation to a wide number of people. There are the polar ends to the position that attract a fringe amount of support, but provide maximum opposition. However, in the middle of the population, the norm, there are infinitely more stakeholders who have an opportunity for input, just not as fanatically. By definition, these moderate stake-holders will always outnumber the polarizing fringe elements.

The right time to invite polarizing groups into the process is at the very beginning. Therefore, 3POI-P thinking begins with defining the extreme positions, views derived from communication with the "fringe." The fringe should not be considered zealots at the extreme limits of each movement, but rather the primary leadership who can articulate a tangible platform. This "fringe" element though generally perceived as outside the norm still delivers the expectations, hopes and goals on behalf of the larger group. This may seem like an odd place to start, but it is essential. Fringe-driven positions are the ones that can best define the group's issues and goals in the clearest terms.

Historically, American government, the party system and American society have directed their efforts to one side achieving victory in an all-or-nothing contest. Think of all the American adages: "Crush the competition"; "to the victor go the spoils"; "the early bird gets the worm"; and "the ends justify the means." US business has thrived on these axioms and reaped tremendous rewards as a result. However, these notions, while creating a competitive environment, ultimately creates a culture of confrontation rather than one where greater achievements could be reached. They are not appropriate axioms for government.

With the onset of the boomer generation, these adages have all too often found their way into our personal lives. How many instances have there been of neighbors fighting over property violations and impinging on each other's "free enjoyment" of their property? This perhaps may not be the best example, but it is symbolic of the change in local communities versus the 1950s and 1960s where neighbors collaborated on putting up a fence or trimming a tree. Part of the goal of 3POI-P was to eliminate this selfish attitude and bring in passionate people and give them the greatest amount of input.

A good example is in relation to the abortion debate. I remember the controversy when I sat down with a Christian right-to-life group and then with the pro-choice group. I got to hear the extreme positions firsthand and subsequently formed the underpinnings of people's views and was later able to clarify and reduce the issues to manageable levels. It also served to remove any previous bias. This is something that the political system prior to 2017 could even come close to doing. The party system necessitated a predisposition against abortion from the right while the left had legal precedent on their side due to the Roe v. Wade Supreme Court ruling. Therefore, no dialogue could be undertaken as each group approached the discussion with a predetermined viewpoint.

The beauty of the 3POI-P approach within the framework of America, is that each of these groups is wholly entitled to their views. One of the odd dichotomies of government prior to 2017 was that the fringe was either ignored as overly-fanatical or listened to way too much because they had the funds to actively solicit lobbyists. Neither situation was terribly fair – fringe groups should have had no more or less influence on government and policy than anyone else. The fringe, or extremists, however are the individuals or groups that express themselves to the greatest degree in society. Ultimately they receive either a disproportionate amount of attention, especially if their cause is seen as legitimate. On the other hand, if their cause is a less savoury one, then they are dismissed as outcasts or kooks. From whichever position the fringe holds, neither is it a balanced approach nor does it represent a sufficient number of people to be considered a way forward.

All that being said, the fringe portion of society still delivers an opinion that quite often is rooted in the deepest logic or the deepest emotional belief. Understanding the root cause of a belief is certainly the correct place to start. Regardless of one's views, the zealots are equally American citizens are entitled a voice in the democratic process.

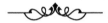

Too often, people start with a bias and then backfill rationale in order to make their opinions justified or seem stronger. It is completely normal for people to have value systems, but this preconceived attitude is generally what leads to conflict, confusion and a lack of open-mindedness in negotiation. In the early 21st century, there often was no valid frame of reference for many of the issues. Take for instance internet law or Middle Eastern terrorism, or environmental issues; no individual or group could develop a definitively correct position. Therefore, preconceived bias generally led to ineffective discussions on just about every social or cultural issue. The world had changed too much for us to rely on past thinking.

In my business days, we quite often would use what is called a zero-based plan. You start with an objective, decide who and what you would need to achieve it, then figure out what kind of budget was required to deliver the objective. At this point, as zero-based plans are often best-case scenarios. You then prioritize the overall objectives and tasks as to which are deliverable and which can be cut away. The key principle though of zero-based planning is that you do not utilize pre-existing programs, thinking or processes in your planning stages. You essentially start from zero and prepare what is considered the best plan to deliver the goal. You can then adapt the plan with existing programs as required or start from scratch, whichever delivers a greater probability of achieving your goals. Would this work in government?

In government, the thinking is supposed to be much more considerate in relation to the number of people, bureaucratic processes and philosophies. Business has a more directional approach and you can get right to work. In government, you are required to be more holistic and the secret to good government is anticipating cause and effect as well as minimizing unintended consequences and maximizing opportunities. Additionally, you build upon existing bureaucracy in order to improve efficiency and to avoid duplicating effort and programs. I agreed with these parameters but felt that these pre-existing conditions were all too often treated as a concrete process.

In our new governmental realm, the right place to start on any so-called irresolvable issue is with a blank page. We decided to face the brutal truth: that the thinking that led us to the current situation was rooted in old thoughts, outdated methodology or political agenda. The prior efforts and thinking had to be removed from the thought-process in order to get a good result. Quite often, this also meant removing individuals who had proven ineffective as well. Plus, there was so much built-in bureaucracy and politicking that nothing could be done even if the old methods were followed. This was one of President Obama's big mistakes -- he tried to work through the existing process rather than ignoring it and proved it couldn't be done, at least not by fair means. George W. Bush on the other hand got things done by being subversive, lying to the American public and essentially defiling democracy. Neither was a good approach to governing.

So on any issue we start with both sides of the fringe component.

The next step: establish what the best-case scenario for each of the groups might be.

The real beauty of the 3POI-process, is that the objectives as stated by each fringe position cannot logically or statistically be pursued, because they do not represent a sufficient percentage of the population. Therefore, neither group's objectives need to be addressed as an absolute goal beyond the initial discussions.

At this point, the next step of 3POI-P requires that we involve experts. Key moderates are recruited, but with a wide mix of positions on the direct issue. The ensuing discussions are not necessarily characterized in terms of negotiations, but rather under the guise of finding commonalities in thinking, objectives and rationale that would be attractive to both groups. When this process is delivered in a spirit of commonality, trust and progress, it is amazing just how quickly resolutions can be identified and drafted. In reality, the biggest and most important part to the discussion process is simply finding people who embrace an intelligent mindset and can discuss objectives without a partisan fanaticism. There are millions of people who can do this when they are properly engaged in the political process.

Under the old party system there were of course lots of smart and intelligent people, but distrust, unilateral gain and inequitable positions of power usually caused the process to fail. Moderates and rational Americans were not attracted to the political system and subsequently stayed away or observed from afar.

Here is a tangible example of how 3POI-P worked back in 2018 on the issue of abortion.

We brought together representatives of various sides and positions for one week in Philadelphia. They were given one week to draft a "Spirit of Law." In that time, they were able to outline common thinking whereby they identified shared objectives.

In less than two days, these three objectives were put forth:

- Sanctity of the life of the fetus in the eyes of God
- Good health and welfare of the mother
- Equal access to medical resources

With these agreed-upon objectives in mind, the experts, through a spirit of trying to resolve the issue rather than enforce their own position, agreed to a draft document that outlined a philosophy towards abortion as well as guidelines for accommodation of abortions when all other avenues have been exhausted by the mother and the resources are locally available.

The perceived toughest objective was to identify the status of the fetus as the creation of God and subject to all the rights and philosophies granted within that term. The interesting point to the draft was that it worked regardless of the religion. The fetus in all cases was acknowledged as a creation of God per whichever religion the parents or nature determined.

Most doctors agree that by week 10 the head is larger than rest of the body due to hind brain development which is responsible for regulating heartbeat, breathing and most muscle movements. Though the groups held opposing positions, both were comfortable at this point that the fetus is now taking on most of the physically functional aspects of a human and as such this was the moment that the fetus transformed from being an unsustainable organism into a human being.

It was then agreed that after sixty days no abortion could be performed under any circumstances. There was only one possible exception after sixty days and that was in the instance of the possibility of a fatal result for the mother. Within the first sixty days abortions were completely up to the mother as long as local resources were available. The fetus would be afforded all the appropriate acknowledgements and rites such as burials and church services and would be funded by the church requesting such actions. However, none of the bureaucratic governmental process that normally goes along with the birth and death of an individual had to be undertaken. It was just common sense that the baby be recognized as a life in the eyes of God, but in the eyes of the state it did not need the same treatment. To the pro-life people this was perfectly acceptable and to the pro-choice they had what they wanted.

As far as the rights of the mother went, they had the obligation to be responsible for their own actions in the first sixty days. Firstly, they had to recognize that they were pregnant, secondly identify if they wanted to keep the fetus and thirdly take steps to pursue the abortion including full payment for the procedure. This was considered mostly reasonable by everyone involved. The pro-choice participants were quite in agreement that most women should know if they are pregnant within that time frame and a decision can be reached soon enough... especially if the cause of the pregnancy was of the unsavoury manner i.e. rape, incest. If the woman seeking the abortion was below the age of 16, she was required to have an immediate family member approve and share in the responsibilities surrounding the procedure.

The issue of having the mothers funding their own abortions was completely agreeable to all parties as well as it was seen very much as a voluntary procedure and one in which a decision was being made by the family involved. It was not seen as something that should be covered by health insurance in any manner. If a private organization wanted to fund abortions they could do at their discretion. However, these private groups would have to prove that federal or state money was not being used to fund the abortions. This was a strict policy. Even in the case of a low income family, if payment was not made prior to the procedure then it was not to be performed.

As the expert panel developed the thinking behind the issue, they also suggested that social services organizations should be more involved with helping the mother find financing or in a more favourable situation, assist the mother in potentially developing an alternative course of action such as adoption. Over time, a fully-funded pregnancy subsidy was developed so that women were able to carry their babies to term rather than going through with the abortion. Upon the birth of the baby, the mother still had the option of keeping the baby and embracing it as part of her family. This for everyone was the optimal solution. There was some small issue at the time that this was an inequitable solution as it was felt that women who chose abortions had to pay while the women who kept the baby were subsidized, but our government dismissed this line of thinking citing the new process that had been utilized and that trying to treat everyone equally was no longer a major goal of the world. I will discuss this equality issue in a later section.

The third stated goal was in relation to having access to medical resources and this also figured prominently into the experts discussions. Maternity care centers were required to provide resources for women to have the abortion under the new guidelines. The intent was to include all pregnant women simply as expectant mothers and within the same group. Women who were considering abortion were required to attend at least one group session prior to their abortion in order to sit and hear discussions regarding pregnancy from other expectant mothers.

The group also developed rationale that if women considering abortions were brought into the same realm of hopeful mothers and other like-minded people who shared their circumstances then they might be able to identify alternatives and in some cases might even choose to keep the baby. This proved to be the greatest achievement of the abortion issue as women were able to meet with a peer group who were very positive and in comfortable situations and reinforced the happiness they felt and put that good intent into a lot of younger women's mind. Also, women would also meet others who shared their predicament and had someone who knew what they were feeling so that they were able to talk to people who understood them implicitly.

Further, the maternity centers became centers for adoption services and became a new source of revenue for the hospitals and they invested further resources into the care and research so that safer and even less invasive methods of abortion were identified and developed. In fact, the word abortion became no longer in use as the stigma of terminating a first sixty day pregnancy evaporated. Today, we know the process just as expectancy cessation. It is very common and has become a huge source of revenue for the hospitals.

Once the two sides got together and saw that by treating people with human decency and that a medical and non-politically motivated solution on the issue was delivered then maintaining an aura of conflict was not necessary. The issue was eliminated from our cultural vocabulary and has basically disappeared over time.

The final step in 3POI-P is to make the on-going discussions and suggested agreements accessible to the general public for their review. One of the greatest parts of democracy is the ability to take the pulse of the land and to reflect the thinking of the majority in the legislation. However, one of the formal tenets of democracy that the USA has espoused is that every citizen has to be represented. A wrong approach, I feel, believing that only those with an interest need be consulted. We redefined democracy to reflect that every "interested citizen" should have access to the process.

It is not a subversive comment to state that not everyone in the USA is equally interested in every single issue. So we abandoned the concept of universal voting and representation.

Which brings us back to the discussion and decisions regarding abortion. We posted our findings on the Internet. Feedback was solicited. The primary goal was to determine if there were any pitfalls in our thinking and where potential future legal issues might arise. That less than 3,000,000 Americans registered and were involved in the discussion and voting was inconsequential. The simple fact that there was now a spirit of openness in government and that there was an attempt being made to be truly democratic in the procedures of government superseded any broader questions.

Surprisingly, the feedback we received was mostly positive and constructive. I figured the lobbyists and the "fringe" would try to dominate the feedback. This of course did happen and the organized groups tried to weigh in; however, as the voting portion was limited to the one-person one-vote aspect, these folks did not make up enough numbers to have significant sway.

Ultimately, when the legality of the legislation was challenged by pro-life groups, the Supreme Court unanimously agreed with this position in their famous ruling in 2019 that established the legality of the direction and the process. In Hitchens v. Nebraska Health Consortium, Justice Clarence Thomas, in support of the defence's position, used the phrase that we all know today. He referred to it as "Engaged Democracy."

Most of the useful feedback we received represented a level-headed response based on the issues rather than the passion. There also was a great desire on behalf of the public to not misuse the privilege of feedback. The American public approached it with trepidation, thinking that they might get into trouble with the government. Trust and privacy invasion were big issues in 2017. Over time, this fear has abated and people now accept the principle that they can offer feedback or ignore a viewpoint if they choose.

I got a lot of initial credit over this policy and wide ranging acceptance of the process and subsequent legislation that emanated out of it. The legislation when approved did not include any riders, had support of both parties in the Congress and was one of the first policies and legislation drafted mainly by interested non-partisans. I appreciate the praise, but I don't deserve the recognition for the success of the legislation. I had absolutely nothing to do with the actual drafting of the law.

Rather, I provided three things: First, I created a forum based on trust, mutual collaboration and progress; secondly, I laid down a process and structure for the discussion to get through the political and bureaucratic nightmare that seems to have held up government for the previous 25 years. Thirdly, we developed the on-line tools and mechanisms to facilitate our modern era of government. Since then, government has thrived and evolved tremendously.

When we had resolved the abortion debate once and for all early on in my term, I came to realize, and forgive my cliché, that nothing is impossible. Humanity is the greatest result to date of God and the earth. Within three months, our government had been able to overcome one of the greatest moral debates of the past 50 years. I use the abortion resolution simply as an example of the spirit that people can bring to any challenge. It was a revolutionary cultural event.

Here is another 3POI-P example. In 2017, another early issue of my Presidency which we resolved was the foreign immigration situation. It was also a very hot topic during my election campaign. We achieved success by taking a fresh approach and a clear, unbiased mindset that had no preconceived solution or agenda.

At the time, most of the Mexican Border States in the US were quite upset with the migrant worker situation and with illegal immigration. Mexican nationalists would sneak into the US with the hope of prosperity or to escape the conditions in their homeland. Arizona had gone so far as to pass some rather restrictive freedom laws targeted towards Mexicans.

It still boggles my mind that we were talking about walls to keep people out, a silly idea that did nothing to address the core problem. The wall sent the wrong message to everyone. How in the world can a solution be reached when there is a wall being built? There is no way to talk directly with someone when you are spending more time demarcating and defining boundaries. And immigrants were still able to cross the borders at numerous unpatrolled points and through secretive means. Yet all through the campaign in 2016, Donald Trump called for bigger and longer walls to be built.

The solution was a difficult one. But following the same 3POI-P methodology of bringing together the fringe that represented the opposite ends of the argument we defined the objectives. We then brought in the experts, representatives from the Council of Mexican-Americans, agricultural businesses employed thousands, state officials from all of the border states, academic experts in the area and international law and of course Mexican and US citizens to hear first-hand from the people involved.

The solution they developed for the illegal Mexican citizen immigration issue was ingenious. Upon posting the initial thinking and receiving democratic feedback, the first thing that the group decided was to stop processing all visas to Mexican citizens for three months in order to install the procedural and bureaucratic changes that were required. Note that repurposing of bureaucracy was a major contributor to the success of all programs that were developed and implemented in this period. Bureaucracy and administration had become inefficient and wasteful and rather than try to implement gradual change, we went for wholesale change.

The fundamental principle became that no Mexican citizen was allowed into the USA without a visa, under any circumstance, but balanced by much easier entrance standards. The process of obtaining a visa was simplified by having just one application form. Applications could be submitted over the internet, through the mail or dropped off at an American consular outlet. Face to face meetings were no longer required. As long as there was no felony record and the candidate was in possession of valid identification or passport, the person was given an approved three year visa and was granted a one-time admittance to the USA for a maximum period of six months within the three year period.

If during that period the person in question found valid employment then that person was required by law to contact the office of immigration in order to have their visa extended. Once again, as long as the people in question were gainfully employed, and not doing anything illegal, then the visa was automatically extended for one year periods. There were to be no investigations.

The owners of the business that were hiring were obligated by law to report their employees. The big difference for the owners was that they were free to pay these workers whatever they wanted. It was a 100% free market. There was no notion of minimum wages or insurance for these workers. However, the businesses were required to exercise the same standard of care, safety and employment law as for any other employee in terms of length of hours, payment of overtime etc. The reformed bureaucracy was part of the process and had the ability to investigate any violation or complaint. They also had the real authority to recommend criminal charges if violations were identified. The bureaucracy was held accountable for monitoring the situation and instilling best practices.

Initially it was absolute chaos.

As I have mentioned before, there was a distinct lack of trust from all parties that the government would be able to deliver and enforce the new way of doing things, especially after just three months. The Mexican citizens themselves were distrustful of business and government and felt they were always one step away from being deported. Businesses didn't want to do the administration. And the bureaucracy did not want to work harder or try a fresh approach. Therefore, the initial launch period was admittedly, a huge mess.

Under these circumstances, most previous governments would modify or blame the other side for the failings of the program. We, however, were to be more stoic than that. We took the criticism, the threats, the call for my impeachment. It only seemed reasonable that change would be resisted. In hindsight, we should have heeded caution and introduced a more gradual implementation of the program. But, we were new in office and wanted to make a difference.

After the initial year and a lot of government pressure on all the parties involved, there were quite a few test cases to create good and bad examples. Stake-holders started to see that the new system could actually do as it was suggested. There was no longer an advantage to abusing workers and the employees began to realize that they were part of the economic community of the USA and ultimately everything started to run a whole smoother. The businesses saw profits due to the quality and hard work of the Mexican citizens. Owners and managers came to realize that as long as they operated fairly and with ethics toward their employees, the government would leave them alone and not impose regulation. The Mexican citizens who were now legally in the US became more and more part of the culture and US economic structure. The bureaucracy came to realize that it was more rewarding and ultimately simpler to institute the program and guidelines rather than continue to deal with so many disputes and poor procedural administration. Ironically, more Mexicans would return to Mexico and work there, utilizing the skills and money they had earned while in the US. By 2024, there were fewer people crossing the border than there was in 1990. It was a testament to the fact that people are generally good to each other; once each side developed a mutual trust and focused on delivering the task at hand they were able to deliver exceptional results.

I firmly believe that with the right approach, the inclusion of the fringe, the involvement of experts and the engagement of citizens, any program can be delivered and be effective. We sometimes as individuals might have a feeling that no one is listening and that I cannot make a difference. The greatest result of the emergence of "Engaged Democracy" is that virtually no one feels that way in 2050. Also, if you don't want to be involved in any governmental activity you do not have to. It is still a free country. However, you don't get paid if you don't get involved.

CHAPTER 5

"CONSTRUCTIVE CAPITALISM"... THERE'S MONEY TO BE MADE IN DOING GOOD

One of my guiding business principles is "Constructive Capitalism." Let's face it; I got rich simply by making the world a better place. That was always my goal from a young age. I'll admit that I also went into business for the recognition, the wealth and the challenge. Despite all that, I operated with a mindset that I would like to build a legacy that would be respected. When my company developed NutrisHouse, which delivered 100% of a person's nutritional daily requirements, I had fulfilled my dream. My legacy was secure. In all honesty, I have far surpassed any dreams I might of had as a youngster.

Upon my company's success in the USA and Europe, we started developing the same food products for the poorer countries. The products for these regions cost one tenth of the consumer-oriented products sold in the USA and Europe, and the flavour was not as good and the packaging was not as elaborate, but the nutrition value was exactly the same. Every single country in the world that imported NutrisHouse Bars saw improved health.

"Constructive Capitalism" is a concept that in essence requires a company to doing something tangibly beneficial to improve the state of the world. This was not necessarily a unique concept, but a progression of the changing consumer-mindset. Prior to NutrisHouse many companies had started to realize that "constructive capitalism" was in their best interest from a business standpoint.

Until NutrisHouse however, genuine corporate contribution was mostly a function of the marketing department. Fund raising or sponsoring a charity run was good enough for a lot of organizations. However, after the success of NutrisHouse, simply writing a cheque to a charitable organization seemed unsettling to most people. Consumers came to expect that if a company does business, they cannot hand over a guilt payment to make them feel better or look good. The contribution must be genuine, involve the resources of the company and be done with the spirit of improving the conditions in the surrounding areas. Even in the USA, the spirit of corporate contribution became more about first-hand infrastructure development rather than continuing to do "fun runs, bake sales and raffles" as I put it in 2007.

The biggest unforeseeable business shift was that consumer preferences changed dramatically with the boomer generation. The previous selfishness of these consumers was still quite embedded but there had been a movement in this group to actually try to redeem themselves before they headed into their senior years. This did not, mean that they were any less interested in looking young, spending on luxury brands and choosing design over function. The "keeping up with the Joneses" phase was never going to let up for that baby boomer group.

However, a trend which I called "yuppie guilt" infiltrated their psyche, and they started to acknowledge the mistakes in their thinking and actions since the 1960s. They had not delivered the concepts of peace and love and as it dawned on this group that their time on earth was dwindling, they decided that it was perhaps time to start giving back. As of course very few could do much individually to this end, they were reliant on making their funds available and started supporting in droves the companies that were involved with real relief efforts and humanitarian causes, demanding that portions of their funds be given to real "on-the-ground" actions rather than just financial contributions. The boomers wanted to know, in order to ease their collective conscious, that the world would see some improvement prior to their death.

As a corollary, the younger generation (known as millennials) were not nearly as selfish in their motivation. They had grown up watching their parents acting like children while the world was somewhat destroyed around them. Most kids by the time they turned 16 were volunteering locally and a great many would take their efforts overseas. Going to Africa to assist in the development of a community turned out to be the equivalent of traveling to Europe for their predecessors. This younger group felt it was absolutely mandatory that a corporation would go on ground in any part of the world where they did business in order to improve the local community.

The bottom line for business of this movement was that they had to become humanitarian in their efforts in order to see their profits increase. Helping people was simply good for business. The era of "Constructive Capitalism" had begun, just not many companies knew it.

One early example of "Constructive Capitalism" came from Lowe's, who shut all their stores in the Southwest US during the Austin, Texas floods in late 2017. As part of their relief effort, Lowe's shipped warehouses full of supplies and sent their staff to the flooded area to start rebuilding the damaged communities. The employees were paid in full their regular salary as well as all of their traveling expenses.

Hurricane Katrina in New Orleans (August 2005) was still a fresh memory in 2017 and no one wanted to see the same thing happen in Austin, so Lowe's mobilized 5,000 employees, delivered untold truck loads of supplies and utilized their management skills to deliver on-ground support to those affected by the floods. Lowe's did not wait for insurance issues, local zoning discussions, or the media.

The effect was immediate and astounding for Lowe's. Lowe's had shifted a big chunk of their marketing budget to fund this effort but certainly reaped the rewards from a business standpoint. Their brand value sky-rocketed as did their stock price following the Austin floods. When asked about their efforts at the time to make such a large commitment, Robert Niblock, their CEO, said that he just could not sit back when he knew he had the resources at his fingers to do something about it. Lowe's was monstrously successful in the South Texas area and he felt that they should contribute as much as possible. Many share holders at the time questioned his decision as they felt that Lowe's was going to receive potentially billions in sales as a result of the rebuilding effort, and that the materials should not have been "given away." Mr. Niblock, however, made it clear to the stock-holders that as a part of the local business community, Lowe's had an obligation to be involved in the rebuilding. His famous line was. "It is not moral to profit from the suffering of our customers."

Today Lowe's has a regular rebuilding program that goes to disaster areas all over the world. They are under no obligation to wait for governmental efforts other than to not interfere with the human rescue efforts.

In the old days of governmental involvement in relief efforts, there was little expertise and efforts were funded by taxpayers. Due to a lack of knowledge, pricing and payment schedules were ridiculously high and rebuilding costs sky-rocketed as companies took advantage of the inefficiencies of government. Corporate America was much better suited to address the immediate problems.

Lowe's was one the earliest tangible examples of "Constructive Capitalism." As a business, they now make exceedingly more revenue by giving back, genuinely and beneficially. Naturally, the other home supply companies have instituted their own programs, but to this day Lowe's, remains the segment leader and by quite a sizable margin.

I, albeit controversially, have always stated that corporations have the most significant ability to contribute to the health and prosperity of the world. Traditional institutions such as government, charity and religion have proven themselves unable to get the job done. These groups have been trying to deal with world issues for years and years but have never delivered any significant impact. The human condition continued to deteriorate in many parts of the world. Government waste and corruption, charitable organizations which spend more on fund-raising than on relief, religious organizations that have lost their way, all have done virtually nothing in the last century to truly improve the "state of the world."

Of course, there have been some exceptions but there really wasn't sufficient will and determination to stick with the efforts. In the past 300 years, corporations are very much the only institutions that have grown and thrived and were expected to continue to prosper and improve. Plus, corporations were also expanding into parts of the world where governments and charitable organizations had no reach. This is fundamental to the notion of change that most other institutions are unable to do. As I have mentioned previously, most governmental systems were established hundreds of years ago and have not changed very much since then. Further, nationalist sentiment does not trust most outside governmental interventionism. Charitable organizations are not coordinated globally and religion is such a variant that no effective solution can be reached. Corporations do not face any of these limitations. I find it rewarding, that companies see the greatest profit through delivering improvements to the world. Consumers have ultimately rewarded the companies through brand value and product purchases.

Now, the people who led the movement were not the existing corporate CEOs in 2016.

In the early 2000s, the ethics of the deal and the value of their company were inconsequential to a great many CEOs and as a result, business ethics virtually vanished. This of course led to the multitude of scandals and the breakdown of the financial system in the 21ˢᵗ century. Looking back, it is amazing just how unethical, unregulated and selfish the American business environment had become.

Those involved in executive management operated with impunity. I am astounded to this very day that, due to the government's financial bailout following the financial meltdown in 2008 caused by Wall Street, only very small numbers in the corporate world lost substantial money, or even their jobs. It was the middle class and the home owners who were hurt the worst.

I had become world-renown for having the utmost ethics in my operations and I think in my own indirect way I contributed to that meltdown in 2008 by being an honest face of American business. I was a poster child for a lot of positive movements and attitudes and I was hopeful that more business leaders might follow my lead. However, this was naive thinking as long as I was a private citizen; but as President it served me well.

Before I go any further, let me state right here, for the record, that I am very much a free-market capitalist. I believe that the market has the ability to grow, regulate, share wealth, help advance the overall economic condition and of course to provide a standard of living that is beneficial to a wide number of people. I do of course also believe that those who own the "means of production" should reap much greater rewards than those whom are in the employ of them. I am in no way, shape or form a communist or, as some of my opponents in the early days referred to me, a "common socialist."

I found it comical at the time that trying to be compassionate while making a profit made you a communist. The business leaders of the day seemed to have had a lot of trouble holding human values towards their employees and their customers, as that kindness was inconsistent with good business. This is not surprising given the overall state of the American business community and the culture that was running it: profits mattered and the effects of actions on people were essentially meaningless.

In business, I had a set of core principles which I utilized in all of my management and with the people I employed. The first thing I held dear was that my business should serve a greater good. I feel quite strongly that corporations should deliver real benefits to consumers and end-users rather than merely exist for the attainment of profits. My core product NutrisHouse was initially developed around the notion that Americans were just becoming too unhealthy in their food choices.

When I developed the original recipe and the biological breakdown process for NutrisHouse, I was surprised with just how little enthusiasm there was for it. I figured I had developed something that would meet all the nutritional requirements of American adult men and women, so it should have been easily accepted. I figured the medical community, the health and nutrition companies, the government and just about anyone else would support this project. I guess wishful thinking makes me the same as every other entrepreneur in their early days.

Of course, I forgot to factor in the reality that none of these organizations, institutions and government bodies would receive any money from my operation so there was no incentive. I was quite dismayed, if not quite a bit upset with the world at large for being so resistant, if not downright hostile to my invention.

When I launched NutrisHouse in 1992, many companies, in the spirit of competitive action went out of their way to impede my success and to put obstacles in place. I thought it odd that a company would spend so much time and energy trying to defend itself against competition rather than trying to make themselves better. This to me is the true nature of competition.

Many underhanded activities were attempted to undermine NutrisHouse, and on a couple of occasions accusations were made against me. NutrisHouse was reported to be cancerous. My food products we full of illegal chemicals that would hurt children. I was accused of running sweat shops in Indonesia even though I did not have a plant there at the time. As a result,

I became disgusted with the actions of many companies and the nature of business in general. I fought back vigorously and withstood every challenge and legal battle.

I definitely believe that corporations must have good motivation and a positive vision and work in a manner that is constructive rather than destructive. I am happy to say that in 2050 most companies operate within that business model; changing the attitude of business is one of the major but less-apparent actions of my business career and presidency. Needless to say, the business community fought my presidential run tooth and nail. When I became president it was satisfying to seek some measure of retribution against companies that had made my life so miserable. Many people considered them personal attacks, and I guess I can admit that in some measure they were. However, the attempts to reform business operations were always substantiated in my beliefs rather than my personal vengeance.

The second value I held critical in my business operation, and which proved to be extremely invaluable when I entered public service, was the continuity of purpose. In business, one of the worst things you can do is change course regularly. Continuity ensures consistency of operations, compounded profits, integrity of process and ease of decision making. Let's face it, if the decision you have to make this week is pretty similar to the decision you made last week, it should be a lot easier to make it and to know how resources need to be allocated towards the achievement of your objectives.

Changing course all the time does nothing but confuse everyone involved. Mostly it confuses your colleagues, as they never know what to be focused on every day. I remember watching Ford Motor Company as they continued their downward spiral in the late 1990s and early 2000s. They changed CEOs, brand positioning, business models and products so often that no one could comprehend what they were about or what they were doing.

By 2009 their stock had dropped to $2.50, astounding at the time for a company of such past grandeur. They were, however able to avoid the bankruptcy actions that both GM and Chrysler undertook in that year.

It took 40 years for Ford to make a comeback to where they were considered a market-leading company again, and they had to switch product categories to do that, becoming a leader in electronics and satellite communications rather than a manufacturer of automobiles. You can of course still buy a new Ford car in all parts of the US – the manufacturing plants are still in operation. However, though you likely do not know it, almost every vehicle in the world, including buses, air planes and tractors, are all equipped with Ford's leading satellite chips and satellite technology. It worked out in the long run for Ford, and ironically it was due to their ever-shifting focus that they were able to fall back on this technology when their autos started randomly catching on fire (again), which in 2019 was the last straw for consumers until their rebound via new technologies in 2025.

My third principle was to represent my company with a great brand promise and then make sure the company reflected that promise in all stages of operations. You can make the case that this works in the opposite manner as well, in that you can identify something within your organization that is a tangible, consumer-focused statement. For example, the vision driving NutrisHouse is what most people world-wide know as our brand positioning of *"healthy souls"*. I genuinely wanted to make a difference in people's lives. Only decisions that were beneficial and supportive of this mindset were the ones we pursued.

Also, inside the organization, everyone I hired and ultimately came to work at our company embodied the spirit of a *"healthy soul"* as well. From our corporate standpoint this meant people who genuinely had confidence in what they were doing for a living but also to have compassion for their fellow man. People of course did not have to be angels, but have a mindset of making the world a nicer place for more than just themselves.

The consumer benefit of "healthy soul" was easy to articulate. Improved health and a corollary improvement of mindset. The overriding premise was that "if one can't nourish themselves, it is impossible to nurture the world."

Of course, I did indeed hope to make some money out of my business and if it went really, really well, and that eventually perhaps it could be a cure for world-hunger. At the beginning though, those were just pipe dreams. But having a single-minded brand vision made it so much easier to choose the issues to stand for and fight over, to choose where to allocate resources, and what *not* to focus on. In my company, if something did not feel right from a perspective of a *"healthy soul"*, we would simply not do it.

So, how did American business have it so wrong?

Many business people back in the late 20th century used to think it was not the role of companies to get involved with domestic culture or politics (other than through lobbying) or anything other than charitable causes, but I always felt that if you did business in a country, you had an obligation to participate in a positive manner.

The biggest difference for NutrisHouse though, was that unlike most companies at the time my definition of a positive manner did not just mean exploiting the locals in order to maximize profits for the parent company. Our company wholeheartedly entered any state/country with the mindset that we were there to operate fairly and if the current situation was dire we strived diligently to improve it. Given the nature of our product, it was not surprising that this proved to be the right course. Few American companies made the effort to improve the human conditions in the country of operation, which led to a series of bad PR events that went against American sensibilities of what is acceptable in business to generate profits. The Bhopal disaster is one, Nike's use of child labor, the fashion industry's reliance on sweat shops and contract labor and a very long list of abuses too voluminous for me to cover here. The guiding premise of most businesses operating in the third world was always to reduce costs and exploit local personnel and physical resources for US home-office benefits. This is of course exactly the same thing that the Europeans had done during international expansion back in the 15th and 16th century, but it was not looked on as lightly under the spotlight of 20th and 21st century morals.

Another huge mistake was the willingness to tolerate corruption and even tyrannical dictatorships. In the 1980s it was not unheard of for the American government to prop up dictators for its own political ends. This mindset in fact continued pretty much up to 2011 when the North African revolutions changed the political landscape in Africa and forced businesses to be less willing to partake in corruption. At the time, corruption in certain countries was kind of a given if you wanted to do business – corruption was just a way of supplementing income since salaries were so low. Bribes and kickbacks were essentially a means of wealth redistribution and companies went along with the bribes and kickbacks rather than try to address the fundamental nature of the issue, the below-the-table economy and the complete lack of accountability in the process. There was a reason that these countries were not prospering despite all the foreign investment; people who held the positions of authority in government and business received all the wealth.

We all know from history that disparate income and wealth will ultimately lead to a revolution. The result -- death and civil wars – cost governments billions of dollars. The foreign community then is in a position of providing aid to help the company from sinking even further. The companies then pull out and take their profits with them while tax-payer dollars are channeled back into the country in question. A backward and unfair situation.

When my company established business in a new country, we would do everything above board. We didn't try to change the structural situation, as we all know it takes time to change peoples' mindset. We might pay a few political contributions initially, but once we started operations, the balance of our attention was spent on the staffers and the vendors that we would be working with. We made sure that these people first and foremost were established in a position of security and comfort.

Our investment was not just in training and developing people, but contributing greatly in providing improved quality of living conditions. Just as in early 20th century America, where company towns proliferated to assist in the well-being of employees, NutrisHouse communities popped up wherever we were operating.

Every aspect of these little communities was paid for by the company and our business partners, and it was all local people that did the work of building the homes and buildings. Supplies quite often were donated. We had a template and proprietary technologies for how the towns should be erected so that roads, plumbing and electricity were easy to start up.

We did not feel that we were trying to manipulate the locals for our benefit, rather we genuinely felt that if NutrisHouse was operating in a region, living conditions were going to improve. I am proud of this legacy.

Many pundits in the 1990s considered my business methods revolutionary, while others characterized them as foolhardy. But what I was doing was no different than what Henry Ford was doing at the start of the 20th century. He paid improved wages, lowered cost of operations and provided appropriate living standards for his employees and suppliers. He contributed significantly to the emergence of the middle class in America and felt that if he created a product that was geared to them and subsequently created a culture that was able to afford it, then growth and prosperity would be the result.

The sad thing about the US business community in the 80s and 90s, which led to the horrible collapses we saw in the 21st century, was, as mentioned before, the complete lack of value that most companies produced. Most manufacturing jobs went overseas in order to produce cheaply. American wealth generation was through finance and real estate. The USA did indeed get richer and wealthier but as many economists have shown, wealth generation without value is unsustainable. At some point, a competitor will come along and start selling what people need and then you are too far behind to catch up. When globalization became the norm and standards increased, the US had nothing to compete with on truly open markets where countries could get goods and services from anywhere in the world.

The professional service sector declined as well due to easy internet access to consultants and expertise from anywhere and everywhere without having to be involved directly with the corporation. Giant companies such as IBM and KPMG virtually disappeared. Computer software became so easy to use that by 2018 anyone could create unique software that served their own specific purposes. There was no need to ever pay someone to do it for you.

Up until 2020, all the only thing the US was leading the world in was developing digital platforms. And the entertainment industry.

Eventually even the manufacturing sector declined. People used home machines to design and manufacture their own products. Companies such as Homebilt and Plastakit grew exponentially. Today, as we know, just about any object can be home manufactured. My wife Natalie designs kitchen dining place settings. Plates, cutlery, candlesticks – just about any accessory you could imagine, selling her designs over the internet. I am proud to say that she does quite well with her business.

During the late 1990s, I was growing my company into Africa and Asia by making NutrisHouse available through private distributors in each region. I never lost focus that my personal gain from these societies would not exceed my contribution. NutrisHouse became the first company to have a "no genocide" policy, refusing to do business with any government that participated in genocide. The secret to my success, was that I was able to side-step dictatorial governments and get my food products to the citizens by dealing directly with the alternative distribution channels that were already there. I never put political policy in the way of delivering proper nutrition. My goal was to feed the poor rather than play games with politicians.

A great example was in Myanmar where the military junta were not going to let my products into the country. Just for context and understanding, there was a tsunami in Myanmar in 2004 and the government's response at the time was to keep out most foreign aid, the rationale being that there were "enough frogs" for the citizens to eat so they did not need aid.

In 2007 when we approached the military government of Myanmar we were offered the opportunity to distribute NutrisHouse through the regular government channels. We were very wary of this direction but we always tried to work with the government first in the areas when we were welcomed. There was no issue initially in dealing directly with them as they paid up front for the systems and in large bulk quantities. Our reputation for nutrition and improving overall health conditions was by now world-renowned and governments were happy when we arrived on their doorsteps. That we improved health in our regions of operation ultimately strengthened a governments' hold on power and up to that point, most dictatorial countries had the mindset that they had to be harsh on people to have loyalty and part of that harshness was keeping the citizens undernourished so that they would not have much spirit to revolt. Giving citizens food made them more loyal. That was an unintended consequence from our perspective.

After about six months though, we realized that of the large quantity of NutrisHouse that had been delivered to the Myanmar government, only 25% had been sent into the population. The other 75% had been resold to other countries that were not in a position to openly negotiate with the outside world (mostly North Korea and Venezuela in 2007). These countries did want the benefits of NutrisHouse but without the requirement of dealing with us directly. The Myanmar resale of our shipment was of course unacceptable to us on two levels.

One. We are a business and wanted to keep control of our sales. Two. The government of Myanmar was being unethical in not looking after their own citizens. On principle of course we were not upset that people in Venezuela or North Korea were receiving the benefits of our products, as someone in need is someone in need, and we had already been paid for the shipment in question. But that could not override our sincere desire that the food go to the people of Myanmar as originally intended. On a basic level, we also did not appreciate being deceived by the Myanmar government, though that was not all that surprising to us, as dealing with military rulers usually involves a fair amount of deception. Government officials denied the resale, but we had irrefutable evidence that this was a lie and in the spirit of trying to overlook one transgression we provided a second shipment, which was promptly sold off without any going to the local citizens. It was a chess game.

We of course just wanted two things. One. The NutrisHouse getting into the right hands. Two. To stop the illegal sales to Venezuela and North Korea as we would have preferred to manage these markets ourselves. We formalized these desires into a formal complaint rather than a legal one. I personally hand delivered it to the President of Myanmar that we were unhappy with the current process. At the time, he merely denied that any wrongdoing had occurred.

Knowing a resolution would not occur within the government, we then entered into a relationship with the Cambodian army, who had strong allegiances with the Myanmar army. Through Cambodian military officials we were able to negotiate a separate distribution deal with Myanmar non-governmental military officers. The reality was that the NGO army regulars in Myanmar were always having to police the populated areas. They were not policing for rebellion, but rather petty crime due to poverty and hunger.

As a result, when the non-government military officers started distribution of the NutrisHouse to local citizens, much of the petty crime went away. They were using NutrisHouse Bars as a settlement mechanism and as a means of keeping the peace. The NGO army officers knew that most of the tribal skirmishes were simply over food so they just fed everybody.

The formal government army officials in Myanmar were of course not happy when they discovered what had happened, but by then the citizens were much more in favour of local military soldiers, and by proxy the government. The NGO army officials were seen as local heroes to the citizens of Myanmar and subsequently any governmental action against these individuals was defended vigorously. The government suspected that if they prosecuted or injured any of the NGO army officials for distributing NutrisHouse, they might face a civil uprising.

Ultimately, we were contacted by the government to see if distribution could go back through the formal government channels and we agreed under the terms of establishing an independent distributor. They had no choice to agree and we selected existing NGO army officials to manage the distribution.

To this day, NutrisHouse is thriving in Myanmar. It has contributed greatly to the overall well-being of the citizens and has lowered domestic expense budgets due to the reduced need for health care services and medicines. The distribution of NutrisHouse has become a major public industry in Myanmar by supplying the needs for infrastructure improvements such as roads, electricity and vehicles. We used Myanmar as a case-study for other less developed nations to show how even in underdeveloped and non-free nations, the health of citizens can be improved once the politics are removed from the equation. Yes, we have been criticized for dealing with tyrants and despots. However, citizens the world over are entitled to a basic level of nutrition. We do our best as a moral institution that these rulers are not able to profit excessively from NutrisHouse or use it somehow to further injure their citizens. We look at what we do as somewhat like foreign aid rather than a consumer product. We provide nutrition first and philosophy second, and look at our operations as a humanitarian effort to help the world.

This approach goes back again to my prior theory of contribution as a means of establishing value. People don't mind spending a little bit more for our products in the developed world as they know that we are actually making a difference.

Of course, NutrisHouse offers great value and a wide variety of nutrition options and flavours. It is designed for a "healthy soul."

Hey, I'll never stop being a salesman.

CHAPTER 6

THE LEGAL SYSTEM...
GETTING TO THE TRUTH AND
MINIMIZING LAWYER IMPACT

The movement towards utilizing contribution as a measure of one's worth resulted in a profound impact on the legal profession and the judiciary. Throughout the latter part of the 20th century and well into the 21st, the legal system had essentially become everything it was intended not to become.

The American legal system was slow, unfair, inequitable and its own version of corrupt. It was extremely biased, fundamentally wrong on every level. Having been a veteran of many lawsuits in my business career, I had first-hand knowledge of just how easily the court system was manipulated and abused to whatever end you might like. Managing the legal system was in fact part of every company's daily activity: you knew legal challenges were going to be launched against you as part of your competitor's on-going activities. Quite simply, managing the legal system was just part of every American company's business plan.

For the most part, individual citizens used the court system entirely incorrectly as well, and it had become all too common to use the court system as a frivolous means of earning a pay check. There were egregious abuses of the court systems, and for whatever reason the court system seemed to exacerbate the situation by ruling quite often in favor of the plaintiffs even when there was no real wrong-doing.

The concept that had pervaded the legal system was that blame had to be attributed in all cases. This is simply not the case and is not the role of the judiciary. The assigning of blame is warranted when something happens to which you can actually attribute blame under the guise that something was perhaps preventable, or was common sense. Blame should not be assigned, however, when one's own actions purposefully bring about a negative result. Even worse were instances where unexpected results or consequences arose that would normally be considered unforeseeable.

Another tenet of early 21st century legal system was the social notion of political correctness and the attribution of blame for almost any action towards some external societal influence. Fortunately, political correctness was a phase, but it nonetheless contributed heavily to the abuses of the legal system and was a corruption of individuality.

In reality, one of the fundamental principles that the rest of the world understood, but which America did not at the time, was that you cannot protect people from themselves. People are going to do things that make no sense and, therefore, other people or groups should not be held accountable for those actions. Companies at the time had to spend millions of dollars trying to warn and prevent individuals against their own ridiculous actions as a means of preventing their products being misused. Having to anticipate all the ways that a product can be misused was a full time job for our legal department.

One famous example from my own business life was in 2006 when an individual from Nebraska had used an empty 20 kg box of NutrisHouse as a doorstop. The person was outside sweeping the step and upon re-entering her house a gust of wind forced the door closed and it hit her square in the face, breaking her jaw in several places. When she sued us, we of course went through all the appropriate legal process to have the case dropped without tying up too much of the court's time. We even offered the defendant $25,000, money which would cover her medical expenses and leave her with a good feeling about the company. Plus, I knew the legal costs would be ten times that amount.

This $25,000 was, however, insufficient to create a spirit of goodwill and we were unwilling to accept any culpability beyond that. It was my personal thinking that the person in question should be held accountable for her own actions. We did not offer any further compensation and were fully prepared to go to court, though we did not expect the case to go to trial.

The fact that this situation ended up in court has stuck with me forever and bothers me to this very day. We presented numerous affidavits, defense of the purposes of the NutrisHouse box, why the box was insufficient to be utilized as a doorstop, and questioned why the person in question thought a piece of cardboard would make a sufficient doorstop. We were ordered to pay the amount of $75,000. Ludicrous, but it taught me about the modern American legal system. The court system had become an integral part of Adam Smith's trickle-down concept at work. Individuals would sue companies for money simply as a means of gaining income.

This event was another influence in developing my notion of individual "contribution." If people expect to get money from doing harm to themselves, the court system should not be a tool in facilitating this occurrence. To me, this was negative contribution, as the individual hindered, punished and prevented organizations from operating. Just ask anyone who worked in the medical sector just decades ago how they viewed the legal system and their patients. Medical practitioners easily spent 10-20 percent of their costs on insurance deriving from lawsuits.

In hindsight, the cardboard box lawsuit provided me with a vehement determination to change the tone of the legal system if I was ever provided the opportunity. Which of course, I was.

The legal system served another, more counter-productive role for America and its freedom by permitting the complete absolution of any individual of any responsibility for their actions. This abdication of personal responsibility was the foundation of the decline of America, and the legal system was at the forefront, accepting any and all cases as a means of attributing blame. Due to the softness of the system and the complete lack of meaningful punishment, people became less and less concerned in terms of punishments and similarly became more and more aware of the possibility of gaining rewards from their poor behavior.

One of my stated goals upon becoming president was to return the legal system to being an institution primarily for punishing criminal activity and corporate wrong-doing.

We ultimately redefined 'illegal' in two ways: 1) Direct contravention of the law and 2) contravention of the "Spirit of Law." With these two tenets in place, we had a much stronger ground to stand on when it came to persecuting criminals.

The foundation of the reform continued to be that all criminals were entitled to fair and equal treatment in the eyes of the law, which is of course no different than what it was designed to do. The court was to be fair, timely, and defend the interest of the individual as it always had. Money, however, would not continue on as the key influencer.

A few basic assumptions had to be reinforced. The most important ones being that the accused was presumed innocent, that a jury of peers would be maintained but redefined to be "genuine peers", and lastly that the concept of precedence was abandoned. Like most events in the 21st century, what had happened in the past was not necessarily the correct way to interpret actions in the present, or potentially the rationale for actions in the future. Also, such a wide range of new techniques and initiatives was possible now in police work that many items considered intrusions in the past were no longer relevant and, therefore, needed to be abandoned.

Also, by moving back to a punishment-focused system, the police forces were able to return to a crime-solving role. Police through the 20th century had become less and less important in the area of crime solving and had been relegated at best to traffic enforcement and dispute resolution. Also, in the period of 2012-2016, police were continuously under scrutiny for racist and overly-violent actions. There were numerous instances where police violence had been captured on cell phones and scrutinized heavily in the media. As a result, police became hesitant for fear of retribution. Having police get back to their core mission was welcomed universally within the fraternity. We started out repurposing of the courts with strong approval from our engaged democratic "3POI-P" methodology. In fact, over 90% of interested citizens were supportive of having a legal system that was efficient, inexpensive and less complex. This support gave us full momentum to take on the challenges that we knew were ahead. The resultant new model made it easier to collect and submit evidence, and a number of restrictions that had hand-cuffed police forces were eliminated. For example, all digital communications were admissible at trial. Trials were conducted in a much more timely manner and the trials themselves were forced to proceed more quickly. Trials would become more black and white, and prosecutors were given more latitude to question defendants.

The impact of lawyers was mitigated on both sides of the equation as they were limited now in the amount of influence. Individuals accused of crimes had to assume a much greater role in their own defense and were required to provide their own opening remarks. Americans believed that if you were accused of a crime then you should have to explain why you were innocent. It was astounding how many cases were resolved in less than an hour – defendants could either explain themselves or not. It did not require hours, months or years to get to the point.

The old tenets of not incriminating yourself hearkened back once again to a time when the meaning of the legislation was completely different. In the 1770s, self-incrimination was much more possible as people seldom understood the law and as a result were often unwilling to testify as the crime they were accused of was not nearly as damaging as some of the other activities they had undertaken.

In today's world though, all accused are expected to testify and be accountable.

The purpose of the legal system was to get to the truth. Determining what happened rather than guilt or innocence became the primary reason for trials and subsequently the system changed accordingly. In the former system lawyers, trying to infer lack of guilt, created shades of gray. In the new legal system, the defense lawyer's role is to help determine the truth. This did, in fact, mean that if you were a defense lawyer, and if your client was guilty, then you could not attempt to disprove it. The court system was never designed so that it could be manipulated to get guilty people out of taking responsibility for their crimes. Defense lawyers became more and more effective in their roles by supplying context and mitigating factors as to why the crime(s) had been committed. There was no need to fabricate scenarios that created "reasonable doubt."

It is ironic that, as America shifted to becoming a more considerate country, sentences became harsher and the penitentiaries less robust and less concerned with offering rehabilitation and training. The punishments were designed to have the perpetrator removed from society and subsequently in the future they would continue to be held accountable upon their release in terms of payments to the victims. We had to create genuine deterrents. We determined that the greatest punishments were removal from their normal environment as well as restitution upon their release. One or the other was not sufficient to deter criminal activity. Both were required.

Sentencing is one area, however, in which precedence was encouraged. The goal was to make sure that similar crimes in similar situations yet in different parts of the country received similar sentences. We did not want to see circumstances where a minor offence in Arizona resulted in extended detention while, in Maine, there was no detainment. Also, there was increased pressure on the system to make sure that all persons regardless of wealth, gender or ethnicity received similar types of sentences. The judicial and legal systems would be truly blind when it came to sentencing.

Violent criminals faced a different sort of punishment. Violent criminals were sent into a separate section of the prison system and removed from societal contact and received systematic, harsh punishment. There would be little tolerance of violent crime; the 21st century was a supposedly enlightened time. Violence towards each other was unnecessary. If a violent crime was conducted in the midst of a non-violent crime, i.e. robbery, then the perpetrators were given a minimum ten-year sentence. There would be no leniency on those that strove to thwart the rules of ownership and personal protection – they would serve as an example and as testimony to the new harshness that would befall violent criminals.

We were of course strongly criticized, but it very much fell within our overall contention that those who contribute the least to society should attain the least in return. We suggested that, if these type of people were so disrespecting of someone else's personal liberty, freedom and property, then that person should not be afforded too much of the same. Life, liberty and pursuit of freedom were only to be enjoyed by those who chose to live by those tenets towards their neighbors.

This philosophy resulted in an unexpected result that I can only now see. In 2016, Americans considered imposing their will and thoughts onto their neighbors and others as an expression of their freedom. Harsher punishments being put to those who infringed on the rights of others, had a similar effect on the thinking of others: people became slightly more concerned about the welfare of their neighbor. This is not to say that a socialist world was created in which people were putting the good of society over their own individual freedom. Rather they were acknowledging that their actions might impact on others and simply took that circumstance into consideration rather than making an immediate decision that was solely individually based.

This thinking had a profound effect on Americans. For example, the fact that one would consider their neighbor prior to mowing the lawn or building a shed made the role of government less necessary at the municipal level. One of the biggest problems municipal governments always had was legislating community building and zoning regulations. When people became more considerate and respectful of their own boundaries, this municipal role became less important and municipal government shrank. Property taxes shrunk dramatically. People realized that, with a little consideration, they could all manage their neighborhood for a greater result rather than relying on a governmental body to do it. Today, most municipal governments manage the infrastructure of their communities. The savings to individual Americans has been in the billions.

White-collar criminals certainly entered the legal system with a different view after 2018. They had their assets withheld, were barred from working again in their field and, as the biggest deterrent, they went to penitentiaries just like other criminals.

When the first few Wall Street brokers were apprehended for violating the "Spirit of Law" doctrines, the community cleaned itself up in a mighty big hurry. It is amazing what people will *not* do when they have a genuine deterrent. The idea that individual gain can be obtained at the expense of others in terms of violation of person or property was becoming a thing of the past. The Wall Street community scrambled towards open and transparent reporting, contributing value through their investments and working towards the "Spirit of Law" rather than trying to circumvent it. The collapse in 2008 was driven by Wall Street manipulation of markets that were based on unsustainable principles. The resulting collapse led to a couple of the companies going out of business, but most survived due to a Federal government bailout of nearly one trillion dollars. Subsequently, Wall Street did little to change their operating procedures nor to change how much money they made. It was not until the Occupy Wall Street Movement of late 2011 that they started to notice that perhaps the way they were operating was not in the best interest of very many people. But even then, the reforms were minuscule.

Wall Street firms instituted a few small reforms and were operating somewhat more ethically until 2018, but with the institution of jail time for criminal wrong-doing including violating the "Spirit of Law" they changed systematically overnight. Just goes to show that real deterrents are what motivate people. People need to be aware that there are consequences for their actions.

This advent of punishment for white-collar criminals was one of the biggest actions that we could have undertaken. Non-violent criminal activity had reached epidemic proportions with few deterrents. Even those who were incarcerated were usually only in jail for less than a year. One of the greatest frauds of all time, the Bernie Madoff ponzi scam, which stole billions of dollars, resulted in a sentence of one hundred and fifty years; however, Madoff spent only eight years in jail.

This outcome was another travesty of the legal system and a reflection of the school of thought that accumulation of money was a valid form of activity regardless of the means and measures that went into achieving it. This struck me as Machiavellian in its underlying principle that the ends justify the means. This is something that I have never understood. Wealth without contribution was meaningless to me. To most Americans, however, easy access to wealth was simply a goal in and of itself.

Along with the reduction in the number of frivolous lawsuits, which had become part and parcel of this "wealth without effort" trend, we banned all lotteries, all development of casinos and on-line gambling. With lotteries and casinos essentially being nothing more than tax-generating initiatives, their real value was non-existent other than as entertainment venues. Lotteries and casinos separated millions of dollars from the people hoping to make it rich. Since the governments at the federal and state level had for the most part balanced budgets by the year 2021, there was no need to continue to collect this tax.

Las Vegas and Atlantic City were exempted from the mandate to eliminate casinos as that was the whole foundation of these cities. Once again, our thought was never to take a holistic approach and deny people access to some of the things they loved in life, but we wanted to make access to these initiatives less about instant wealth. Too many people in America were trying to get rich quick, so we genuinely set out to revert to the traditional American philosophy of Work Ethic. Earn your future through contribution. We did not go after localized sports pools. No one is concerned that you are in a sports betting pool as that contributed to the enjoyment of sports. Gambling in and of itself was not considered a problem; the fact that people used it as a means of a "wishful income" was.

Obviously, the reduced proceeds from gambling produced a downside of this initiative. We instituted a proviso to all casinos that a portion of their earnings must go to the education sector of their state. The number was set at 3.5%, and you would have thought that America had been attacked by the greatest catastrophe in our entire history. It all became a bit overwhelming at times. There was a tremendous backlash by everyone, including the public and the state legislatures, who were the main recipient of the revenues, which I thought they might be happy to see. Well they of course were happy to receive the funds, but they disliked how the spending would be implemented.

Now America is a free country and should be exempt from too much government involvement. However, part of this notion is that everyone should be provided for in some manner and that, though individual freedom is paramount, it is also systemic that some type of infrastructure be put in place for the benefit of all citizens. This has long been a contentious issue for America; we originated in the laissez-faire attitude of Europeans who simply wanted to be free to make a living apart from the noble class structure of Europe at the time. Money became more important than class and this is fine, and I whole-heartedly agree with the ability to further one's personal standing in society.

It was now apparent that, instead of a traditional hereditary-class structure, there was a financial-class structure evolving where those who had funds had access to health care, education, legal systems, business success etc., while those not part of the wealthy classes still had access to these same things, but from an inferior starting point.

Statistics showed that primarily middle class and upwards were able were able to generate sufficient wealth to truly benefit from our great country. However, class limitations kept people in their place. This class separation had become more and more pronounced since the 70's when private schools started to attract all the best educators while the public schools sank tremendously in quality due to poor funding and ineffective administration. The public school system should be as good as any private school. Access to a strong educational system is essential for the future growth and well-being of the US, and this is why I targeted gambling funds. Many people did indeed agree with me on this point, but even those whom were favorable opposed to how my government went about trying to implement it.

At first, we followed the usual "3POI-P" approach of talking to the fringe to obtain our objectives for moving forward. Then we got the moderate experts and interested parties involved so that they could develop legislation and a funding model that would lead to improvement for the public school system. Many areas were looked at for funding, but one of the things that kept coming up was the amount of cash that was flowing through the gaming system. Governments in 2017 were relying heavily on tax revenue that stemmed from lotteries so we figured people were used to gaming being seen as a form of taxation. The thing we didn't see coming was that we were seen as taxing player's winnings and losses rather than taxing up front with the hope to achieve winnings as lotteries do. This was a fundamental difference to the players and one we did not recognize at the time. We met opposition at all levels but the protests that sprang up all over America and the national rallies conducted in Washington soon gave me pause. Being a bit too smug, I chose to persevere and thus began a battle for the next 14 months that ultimately led to the bill being defeated, and me carrying a bit of baggage over a policy that, for all its good intentions, missed the mark. I should have listened to what Americans wanted on the matter.

Why was I so stuck on my position? For one, I wanted Americans to focus more on contribution than on selfish wealth-fulfilling tasks. I think gambling might serve to be wealth-fulfillment, but it is also much more than that, as I think it is part of American culture. If you equate gambling with risk-taking, then this is a fairly easy argument to make. Every person who has ever come to the USA as an immigrant has taken a giant risk to change their life. Many of them left behind everything they had and came to America, to live the American dream and make some measure of personal success for themselves. The parallels with gambling are obvious.

The bottom line was, taxing people's winnings was simply unacceptable. Casinos were already taxed at a higher rate than other businesses. The reaction did not surprise me, because at the time society had not evolved enough for the casino owners to realize that brand contribution was a good business initiative. I stood up many times and made public speeches during this period that I look back on now with a bit of humility. In my rationale, just about every program that I had attempted, and the government had tried, had worked well in spite initial opposition. I was feeling a bit cocky.

What I learned though from trying to pursue this program, regarding the taxation of gambling winnings, was that whether I was standing up to change the structure of government or to expand its role in terms of redefining American values, resistance was to be expected from the part of society that would benefit the least. What I came to be more cognizant of was when policy or initiatives that were perceived to impugn on individual Americans' ability to earn money or was seen as too much government meddling in their daily lives, then the opposition would be broader and more sustained. One speech I made regarding the value of children in our society, and their impact on the future, underpinned just how much I had missed the mark in the instance. Here is an excerpt from a speech I made at a school in California in late 2017.

> *Children are indeed all we have to look forward to as Americans. Our personal lives will be what they are, but our ability to sustain long-term leadership will only happen two ways. The first will be by setting a good example of what it means to be a contributing American, and the second is the education they receive in school. Our role as parents is to establish in our children a spirit of American values that will lead to a strengthening of values through their actions and their contributions. The role of the school system is to reinforce those values but also supply the tools for our children to deliver.*

Even as I read this today, I can't believe how this speech was framed so much that it could easily have been from Communist Russia in the 1920s. The usage of work analogies and such a stock in universality of education was a real mistake on my part, one I fully acknowledge. People accused me of being a radical; of course, my historical situation made this a foolish assertion. What I did do horribly wrong though was to put so much faith into the education system as a foundation of America. Similarly, the use of education to support American values struck me as a form of propaganda.

This again is the beauty of the system that was put in place in terms of "Engaged Democracy" and its appeal. I had to take a beating in the public eye, as did the government, so that the process had some credibility. The fact that the legislation was eventually defeated and almost got me impeached did mean that the process was working and that Americans saw what it meant to be truly democratic. If the president needed to be reminded of their role, then that was part of the process as well.

One of the tenets of the founding fathers was that no one individual should wield authority over the freedom of America. What had happened through the early 21st century is that the president and the parties had indeed taken on a much too authoritative posture and that initiatives were being undertaken that flew directly in the face of the freedoms Americans had enjoyed since their nation's inception. This return to a true democracy, where the voice of its citizens had the ability to determine the rules that affected them, was truly a great day. Despite all the personal negativity I endured, I am glad that it did happen – it showed everyone in America and around the world that freedom was going to rule over money, power and authority.

January 14, 2018, the date that bill was defeated by the American public, is considered the formal date of the rebirth of American democracy and is held up by the current generation of Americans as a national symbol of freedom and democracy as much as any of the revolutionary period's notable days. Currently, there is legislation moving through government to make "Democracy 14" day a national public holiday.

It is ironic that I am referred to as ff21st while "Democracy 14" is a day that exists due to the direct opposition of me. The wonder of democracy. In fairness, the opposition was targeted more at me than the legislation, but you get the point. It similarly shows Americans that no matter how authoritative, or popular one leader might be, democracy will supersede that appeal.

Let's get back to the legal system reforms. Lawyers, in general, had allowed their industry to get out of hand in the late 20th century. There was no sense of law in what they did and ultimately there was a distinct lack of contribution, many felt even a lack of ethics. In my opinion, lawyers sucked more value and goodness out of American culture than any other group or professional sector in history.

Lawyers had taken the concept of right to defense and due diligence to overshadow any other aspect of their being. Right to defense meant doing anything and everything possible to create a measure of doubt in the minds of the jury. In worst case scenarios, they went as far as to corrupt the entire spirit of the legal system. This situation of course was vehemently opposed by me as I could never see the value of taking advantage of weaknesses in the system just to utilize that as a defense. Also, there was the need for judges and government to correct the weaknesses in the system, rather than just exacerbating them and making the weaknesses even more pronounced, such that it became an open flood gate for inequity.

At the time, the premise of defendant's rights was far more important than the victim's rights. A gross betrayal of citizens by the legal system. I fully support the notion that all people are equal before the law, but the victims have already suffered some type of injury and, as a result, should not be subject to increased harassment during the trial phase. Hence the emphasis on punishment and retribution for crimes committed focused on the accused. The victim should always have a sense of justice and compensation upon a guilty finding.

As with the deterrence for frivolous lawsuits by citizens, lawyers who participated in bringing forth a frivolous lawsuit were penalized within the context of the legal system itself. The American Bar Association, which was responsible for regulating the conduct of its members, came to embrace a position of contribution when they put in place a scholarly and principled individual to deliver this mandate. They devised a system whereby contribution was a measured quality. Along with the new measurement criteria, lawyers were graded within the ABA by their competency across areas of expertise. This ultimately led to the legal standards for compensation as well as an access point for people who had been victims of criminal activity.

This rating system was developed so that lawyers who brought forward legitimate cases and argued them in the context of the law and instituted new thinking in terms of the statutes were graded the highest. Lawyers who brought forward frivolous lawsuits, argued them in context of non-legal issues and relied on precedent, were summarily given lower scores. Their compensation then came to reflect their ranking.

The abandonment of the rules of precedent needed to happen in order for the system to move forward especially in the area of trial law. Many people in the 21st century, me included, believed that every single incident was different from the one before. To me this extended well beyond the justice system and was also applicable to just about every aspect of human life.

In the early 21st century, the world had gotten so complex that it was nearly impossible to turn to the past for guidance on just about any issue. History had never seen a world in which instant communication was possible, a world where global considerations had a real-time application, and a world where there were numerous competing interests. Let's face it, the history of the world will be as vastly different in 2100 as it is now in 2050, so there is no point relying on our legal opinions in the future. We have to write our own future and look beyond history. With the 21st century seeing cases of terrorists, violent criminals, domestic abusers, pedophiles, drug sellers, white-collar criminals etc., the legal system, as early as 2020, started evaluating crime within a greater perspective.

The issue on trial became the definition of intent and context for the crime as grounds for punishment, rather than the act itself. This is why precedence became completely meaningless. The system will never be able to contextualize a crime in the same manner across two separate incidents. This is truly a more accurate way to dole out justice than with precedent; it treats every case and more importantly every individual as separate and, from an even greater perspective, equal. Therefore they would receive a fairer trial as well.

Context replaced motive as the driving force for trial and evaluation of criminal activity. Let's take a hypothetical example whereby by a financier purposely sets out to defraud their company of funds. The person is stealing from their employer and should be given a jail sentence for his actions. As a parallel crime, a local employee at a suburban restaurant removes money from the till. Well, utilizing a context methodology, the two are both stealing and will receive a similar punishment. There is no distinction made between the nature of the crime; rather, the intent and context of the crime are the primary determinants of punishment. Some consideration might be given to the scale and scope of the amount, but there should be no difference in punishment for in stealing $20 or $2,000,000. We shifted the thinking to contextualize theft in terms of value. For example, if $2,000,000 represented 1% of company assets as did the $20, then the criminal act of robbery was considered the same in terms of sentencing. Motive did not matter.

With violent crime, intent and context, rather than precedence, can be utilized to determine appropriate culpability. For example, a street fight that leads to the death of one of the combatants as a direct result of the opponent's assault is not considered murder as the context of a street fight is not usually to bring about death, but simply to defeat the opponent. Even in the instance where the person who died was knocked to the ground and received life-ending injuries, that is not seen as murder as the intent of the combatant was not to kill his opposition. The victim entered the combat willingly and with the same intent and context of his opponent. Therefore, it's not murder. Punishment would be negligible in these circumstances.

However, where weapons are introduced into the combat the context changes. Anyone who uses a weapon in a street fight clearly has escalated the amount of injury that he wants to impose on his opposition and is, therefore, subject to a different interpretation in the eyes of the law. In this instance, once a foreign object of any kind is introduced into the fight and a death is the result of the use of that foreign object then the charge of murder is able to be introduced as the intent to inflict serious injury is clear and can be assumed to be the intent of the combatant. It cannot be argued as self-defense if a weapon is used and the victim did not possess one.

The intent of the reforms was to overcome the abuse of the legal system, not by citizens, but by lawyers. The goal was to have lawyers simply make a fact-based and truthful argument of the incident in question. As I have mentioned previously, lawyers had swung so far into a world of arguing non-fact-based arguments that rarely were the facts of any case even presented. Couple this with the mandatory testimony of the accused at trials and we were usually able to arrive at a correct conclusion of the crime and in much more timely manner.

This "correct conclusion" of a trial was a concept that had gone away from the court system in 2016. There, in fact, were very few instances where lawyers tried to ascertain what happened; rather they preferred to create confusion or justification. This seemed to be everyone's defense in a criminal trial in 2016. It is blatantly the fault of the trial lawyers who found that the simplest way to win a trial was to create a question of reasonable doubt rather than a statement of truth. The lawyers, by fabricating imaginative defenses, had created a system where the courts were no longer a deterrent for criminal activity, as the accused knew that an argument of innocence could be formulated under any circumstances, and that they could be exonerated, regardless of actual guilt or the nature of the crime.

This downfall of the court system, this utter contempt for personal accountability, was at the root of America's collapse at the start of the 21st century. Overhauling the entire court system was crucial to reinstalling a sense of accountability.

Forgiveness is at the heart of every Christian country and is part of the American ethos. However, forgiveness should not mean lack of punishment. One of the tenets of the new judiciary was to increase punishments for criminal activities. Short sentences and reduced prison times were certainly a reflection of America's forgiving heart, but the result was too traumatic in terms of the national identity. When no one would be without fear of severe punishment, individuals willingly took risks to gain their own desires over those of others. Resorting to murder and violence to attain them was pretty common in the early 21st century.

Through the implementation of intent and context, and abandonment of precedence, and a move towards finding the truth, the judiciary and the legal system were now able to take a fresh look at how trials were conducted and were subsequently more focused on obtaining the truth of the events rather than creating an element of reasonable doubt. This effort did not in any way undermine an individual's rights, rather it fairly balanced the rights of the victims with the rights of the defendants. Once the focus of trials was repurposed, the judicial system became much more efficient at determining guilt and innocence.

Coupled with the "Spirit of Law" and the new scoring system for lawyers, those that were best at determining the truth, intent and context became more in demand and subsequently received more compensation and respect. It also served as a greater deterrent for criminals, as they knew there was a much greater chance that they would, in fact, be found guilty so crime rates started to decline for the first time in a long while.

Reforming the legal system to one which prioritized truth and punishment over all else, was a cornerstone to America becoming a responsible nation. Individual citizens learned that personal accountability is an integral part of individual freedom.

One final topic I wanted to touch on in relation to the legal system was in the area of family law.

The greatest change was the introduction of "termed" marriage licenses.

The policy of termed marriage licenses was an extremely good one. I viewed it at the time as a bit reprehensible in my heart, but the state governments could not overlook the will of the people. The idea of termed marriages worked out to be perfect on just about every level. As divorce rates by 2025 had grown to almost sixty percent, there seemed to be no point in marriages being considered for a life term anymore. It just wasn't the way that families in America were structured.

The primary benefit was that the inevitable strain of being in a marriage was alleviated. There was no need for a messy divorce as people knew that they could just wait out the current term of their marriage and that would be the end of it. Of course, messy break-up of marriages were not a thing of the past nor will they ever be, and the dilemma was even greater when both parties did not want to part to the same degree. However, that was no different than what was going on prior to the termed licenses so it didn't matter all that much in my mind.

The primary benefit of the termed marriage licenses was the reduction of costs of legal fees. Divorce law was a huge business and usually the biggest cost incurred during separations. Since the settlement was now predetermined as part of the marriage license, legal expenses became moot. By 2035, hardly anyone went to court anymore. Initially, there were many marriage licenses that were called into question when the marriage dissolved and it was primarily by the person who had not increased financially as much as the other.

The termed marriage license required a list of independent assets as well as the expected financial positions for each partner throughout the balance of the marriage. There usually was a willingness on both parties to share matrimonial assets that grew (or shrunk) over the period of the license and that was agreed upon at the time as well. Whatever amount in either hard cash or percentages of assets was agreed upon, was what rewarded at the end of the license period. A great deal of the time it was 50/50, so in practice, very little changed. Where there was a substantive improvement in the dissolution phase was where one party had a disproportionate amount of assets at the outset. These divorces were now settled in no time and the parties involved could get on with their lives.

The term periods of the license was as follows: If one of the persons involved was in their first marriage the period was 7-1/2 years in duration. All other licenses were for five years. Renewal of your marriage license was automatic for a five-year term if no termination request was received. After the second renewal of a license i.e. 12-1/2 years of marriage, an update to the asset list had to be submitted.

Similarly, the notion of common law marriages was completely abandoned. Couples that lived together without a marriage license were not entitled to any assets other than their own personal ones. This meant that if a couple were together and did not register a marriage license and then they broke up, there was no such thing as palimony or financial compensation to either. The thinking was that as traditional relationships were being abandoned then so should the common-law approach. The couple was either building a life together, which in this case meant you were married, or you weren't.

The bottom-line was that marriage licenses were no longer seen as an emotional type of agreement but rather a legal one. It made sense that everyone entering a relationship, that might potentially end, it was better to address this scenario up front with clarity, rather than after the fact when emotional and vindictive thinking and legal posturing would be paramount.

Not surprisingly, the termed marriage licenses caught on like wild fire and in the first year, over 15,000,000 licenses were registered on-line. It only took about thirty minutes on-line as long as you had your asset inventory (which was updatable as required). There was no need to go to a church, hire a lawyer, and register at town hall or even say "I do" if you didn't want to. We were quite kitschy in having both parties click on an "I DO" button as a form of agreement to the terms of the license they were submitting.

People were still welcome of course to hold their wedding ceremonies as they chose. However, those were of no legal consequence.

To end the marriage it was as equally simplistic. When the period of your license was coming to an end, either party just had to go into their file and file a notification that they marriage was to be dissolved. Case closed.

Of course, there was likely to still be bickering between the parties involved and whether the assets were allocated as stipulated. The good thing, is that these were no longer the concern of the government. Some things in life people just have to do on your own.

I have searched high and low around the world for what might be a good solution to the issue of child custody upon marriage termination, when the split was not amicable as per accepted terms. Both parents most of the time want the children to be with them. The states have tried to avoid any policy that go into the area as it just seems like an area for government not to be involved in.

In hindsight, I guess it might be appropriate, as legislating the future of children is a moral issue. However, as then, there are still way too many custody battles in the family courts and though we have pretty much gotten rid of the anger and disputes that arise out of asset allocation, we have been unable to stem the emotional and hurtful pain of child separation when the marriage ends.

The one provision that we have been able to put into place is that if any children are over the age of sixteen, they get to have the biggest say in the decision in terms of where they will stay, if they want that choice. Many children, it was found, do not want the responsibility of selecting which parent to stay with while others welcomed it. Therefore, we decided to give the older children more say in the result. Children younger than sixteen are of course consulted in the balance of the cases but don't have as much influence over the outcome.

Finally, when it comes to children, both parents are equally responsible for child support until the child turns 18. There is no recourse through the courts. As with the marriage contract itself, both parents become 50/50 responsible for the welfare of their children. It is up to the two of them what economic condition the children will grow up in.

Fortunately, many private organizations have evolved that are capable of increasing the standards of families. As I referred to earlier within the new era of "Constructive Capitalism" companies have spear-headed numerous initiatives to make sure that children are being fed, getting an education, receiving healthcare and not living in sub-par conditions as a result of to their parents economic condition or lack of a personal relationship.

The way people live their lives is certainly not the business of the nation's government. Many people have put forward an opposing opinion on this issue over the years, but to me, this is the ultimate individual freedom. The ability to live your life and raise your children without outside regulation.

CHAPTER 7

JULY 4, 2022...KENNEDY AND NEWFOUNDLAND JOIN THE UNION

The creation of two new US states on July 4th, 2022 is the single greatest legacy economically and militarily of my term as president. With the purchase from Canada of the eastern portion of their country, which included Eastern Quebec, the provinces of Nova Scotia, New Brunswick, Prince Edward Island and the island portion of Newfoundland, the USA headed into a period of growth and prosperity due to the expansion of American businesses, expansion of military resources, acquirement of natural resources, increased shipping capabilities and the ingenuity and passion of these new American citizens.

In hindsight, it seems ridiculous how easy the purchase of foreign lands were for the US, especially with so little fanfare and resentment of the international community. But firstly, the area we were purchasing was of little consequence on the international stage, and secondly the provincial governments and their citizens were so disillusioned with their Canadian federal government following years of austerity that they were overwhelmingly in favor of the purchase.

Just a quick history recap: the states that we all know in 2050 as New York, Vermont, New Hampshire, Kennedy and

Newfoundland were all different prior to July 4th, 2022. New York State was extended on its eastern border to include the city of East Montreal. Vermont was extended north to the area across from Quebec City while New Hampshire's borders were extended following the border with Maine to Riviere du Loup. Maine received a tremendous benefit by receiving all the land north of Kennedy to the opening of the St. Lawrence Seaway.

The region that was formerly referred to as the Canadian Maritime Provinces (New Brunswick, Nova Scotia and Prince Edward Island) became one all-new American state known as Kennedy. The island portion of the former province of Newfoundland and Labrador became the state of Newfoundland. Labrador remained in Canada and became part of Quebec. The island known as Anticosti, which sits at the entrance to the St. Lawrence River, was split evenly with the northern part staying as part of Canada and the southern portion becoming US territory as part of Maine.

Maine ultimately became the primary area for investment and shipping routes for the St. Lawrence which was shared fairly and equally with Canada. That we purchased these areas for Cdn $1.2 trillion dollars (approx US$750 billion) still amazes me, considering the prosperity and ingenuity that the region has shown. The Newfoundlanders and Kennedyites, as new American citizens, have become role models for the rest of Americans on how to live in a peaceful and orderly manner. They continue to embrace an unforeseen hospitality and demonstrate to the world a fair amount of empathy for overall society at large. The 51st and 52nd states of the United States of America have become not only stellar examples of US society but have also been recognized as idealized societies around the world.

So, why did Canada sell part of their country to the USA? Well for the first time ever here is my perspective.

Following a series of exorbitant spending sprees early in his first term, Prime Minister Justin Trudeau's government was in a state of monstrous debt as of 2020. When he took office in 2015, Canada had a balanced budget and just about $700 billion dollars in federal national debt. Within 18 months Canada had a federal national debt that exceeded $1 trillion. Within three years that amount had ballooned to over $1.5 trillion. The Federal Liberals were beginning to make cuts to programs across the country and in the process turned most of the provincial governments against them. The health care system took the greatest hit, and in Canada this was the "golden egg" that Canadians were unwilling to part with.

What was even more of a catalyst was that, through a series of tax initiatives, the health care system had been reduced without public dialogue and it had been revealed that surgery for cancer treatment was being denied by many hospitals as the stipulated direction was to utilize chemotherapy and medication. This circumstance first became known to the Canadian public in February of 2018, and by summer the full magnitude of the story was causing much public uproar. To Canadians, meddling with their health care system was tantamount to treason.

Further a series of missteps took Canadian citizens by surprise. Justin Trudeau had campaigned on fairness, openness and political reform. But as his government became mired in debt, none of these promises came to fruition, and despite some early success upon election, he was reverting back to the clandestine world of secret politics. Canadians were not happy.

Canada's founding documents instill a mantra of peace, order and good government and even though they had their issues, their expectations were mostly in terms of access to services. Income and sales tax were much higher than in the US but people, in return received health care, a good infrastructure, clean utilities and access to an abundance of natural resources that kept prices reasonable. Their business community had access to US markets through the Free Trade agreements and was thriving nicely, having even weathered the global finance collapse of 2008 due to their more restrictive banking policies and their citizens' ability to manage their individual debt to a greater degree.

However, as mentioned many times before in regards to the US political system, the Canadian political establishment suffered the same paralysis. The driving reason for political existence was political expediency rather than public service. As a result, this led to a great number of governments that were unable to maintain power and subsequently resulted in numerous elections. Canada had much more political variance than in the US, but it was based as much on geographical splits within the country as it was on philosophical goals. For example, Quebec had a unique political party called the Bloc Quebecois which only elected candidates in their province. The New Democratic Party, left-wing in its views, was represented mostly in downtown urban areas and on the west coast. The other two national parties the Liberals and the Conservatives alternated leadership and were the only two parties that had ever put a Prime Minister into power. However, these two parties were more often seen as replacements to each other once the other had lost favor with the electorate rather than a clear and definitive preference by the voters.

As the election was looming in 2019, Trudeau was in danger of losing power and most parts of Canada had turned against him. Being a native Quebecker, he had particularly alienated those in his native province, and as a group they were threatening to separate from Canada if he was re-elected. Quebec's departure from Canada felt inevitable.

In order to get out in front of Canada's break-up and his election loss, Trudeau contacted me directly to see if there was anything that could be done in terms of increasing US revenue coming to Canada. He figured that an infusion of cash might limit the further debt as well as having investment boost the economic area. He also planned for the majority of those funds to go to Quebec as a means of getting some measure of electoral support.

Ironically though, the citizens of Quebec, who had always supported the Bloc Quebecois, their own political party at the federal level, voted overwhelmingly in favor of the Liberals in 2015. This was seen as a demonstration of the politics of dissent. In the previous election in 2011, they had voted in a series of NDP candidates. They had even gone as far in some ridings to vote in candidates who had never even set foot in their ridings, nor did the candidate even speak French. It was a travesty of democratic principles, showing once again that representative democracy did not reflect the world. Note: "Engaged Democracy" caught on as well in Canada in the mid 2020s.

One final event in early 2018, one that kind of tipped the scales, was that the Russians began making gestures towards the Arctic, making claims for territories in what was then the Canadian north. This situation never became widespread public knowledge, but the international community was certainly aware of the situation and there was universal condemnation of Russian expansionist actions. Naturally, Americans have tremendous interest in the Canadian north as we had many established military bases there and utilize the shipping lane of the Northwest Passage to connect the Atlantic and Pacific oceans. We did not want to see anyone jeopardize this access nor did we want to allow the Russians to circumvent international law.

By 2018, Mr. Trudeau had to face the nation and state that Canada's public debt had exceeded five hundred billion dollars. Now this may not sound like a lot to Americans, who were used to trillions of dollars in debt at the time, but in Canada fiscal conservatism is much more part of their culture. To the electorate, being in such a large negative position was unacceptable.

Mr. Trudeau, facing an election in 2019, ran on the platform of rehabilitation of his poor fiscal management. Surprisingly, the Canadian electorate agreed with him and re-elected him with another majority government. Trudeau is a tremendously likable person and had a great reputation on the international stage. I have to admit, it was a terrific bit of politicking to retain his government and I respected him for that. On the other hand, as much as I like him personally, I did not admire his governing ability. I fully admit that I was quite dismayed as well that a key western figure could govern in such a reckless and malevolent way that had cost his country so dearly. Ultimately it cost Canada a portion of their country.

As president, I came to know Mr. Trudeau quite well and I have to say that I liked him. He was a good tactician in managing the political process and a relatively straight-forward politician who understood the pros and cons of policy in terms of foreign governments. However, he was much better at international relations than he was at running a government.

We became strong allies and I would suggest he was a tremendous advisor and ultimately a friend. One thing I always envied about Justin was just how small his entourage was. Whether he was traveling abroad or at home he was much more relaxed than I ever was. I was always surrounded by body guards, members of Congress, lobbyists, media people and my staff. I understood that mine was the most powerful seat in the world and of course I had many more enemies than Justin, but I wasn't sure in my heart that I was any more vulnerable to a personal attack than he was. I had already lived through one assassination attempt, so had very little fear of a second.

I remember the day the discussion about Canada's budget surfaced. We were in Bern, Switzerland, for a conference and were having dinner together, which was a rarity. His biggest issue, he mentioned, in terms of his national agenda, was dealing with Canada's massive debt.

As I mentioned, Canadian citizens were not nearly as affected by the recession as we were in the US, due to lower individual debt issues that most Canadians believed in. Generally, Canadians did not buy homes beyond their limits, they didn't buy things they didn't need, they liked to pay off their debt on time and in full, all while paying much higher income and sales taxes. It would only make sense that, in a debt-averse area like Canada, there would be pressure to have balanced budgets if not an outright surplus.

Since we had had considerable success in lowering our national debt during the first three years of my presidency, though it was still ridiculously large, I suggested doing one of the things we did – sell off a few of our core assets. We sold off some of our military capabilities to the private sector and raised nearly $50 billion in the process. Previously we had sold American Samoa to Australia and that worked well for us. This had been a $1.5 trillion deal and when combined with the tax reforms it changed the future of both our nations as it lowered our debt dramatically and allowed us to start buying back some of our bond issues, which were the main reason that we were losing out economically around the globe. By paying down so many of our debts within one 90-day period, the US dollar sky-rocketed to heights that hadn't been seen in 50 years and so further strengthened US business that it gave us a sizable advantage within a small time frame. I remembered even thinking, while explaining some details to Justin, that maybe we could help him out with a land purchase. I was sincerely joking at the time.

The other area enhanced from this financial turnaround, was that the American pride and ingenuity that had been such a huge component of the "STAND UP AMERICA" campaign came to life and was reinforced in the hearts and actions of American citizens. The "Made in America" stamp became world-famous again and branding of US companies thrived overseas. Also, Americans, in droves, felt confident in the markets and started going back to a more tangible way of investing which was investment in companies that contribute and provide value rather than merely speculating. Speculation was dead, given the crash of the market in 2008 as well as the substantial losses seen after the Japanese earthquake and nuclear accident in early 2011. The final straw was the decline of the Euro in 2017 when trillions of dollars of investment capital was wiped out in one forty-eight hour period. As a result, most investors would not take the risk to speculate anymore.

Also, given the changes to regulation and the "Spirit of Law" guidelines that brokerage houses had embraced, there were not as many financial products available for sale. Further, as money had become much more a tool of valuation, people didn't want speculative investment gains as much anymore as it was seen as sourced from lack of contribution.

Later, during a separate meeting, Mr. Trudeau was commenting on the immediate benefits of the sale of American Samoa and was curious to know if maybe the US would have interest to perhaps be a buyer rather than a seller in a deal with Canada? I smiled and just said "let me know what you are thinking" and left it at that. To be honest, the thought of expanding the US geographical boundaries had still then never entered my mind. The 50 states and other holdings were sufficient for us to thrive. Plus, due to the issues of nationalism the notion of buying domestic foreign lands seemed quite odd. However, my appetite for growth spurred my inner resolve to have America be the biggest and best, so the concept started stirring in the back of my mind.

On my first serious look at Canada, the ideal scenario was to gain control over a big chunk of the northern areas so that we would have territorial claims to the Northwest Passage, a military presence all along the northern borders of Russia, and access to all the water we could ever want. We already had a presence in the area with Alaska so it would make sense for America to extend it reaches and infrastructure throughout the north.

The second area I looked at was the west coast, including the Rocky Mountains and northern Alberta. This would mean one of Canada's largest cities, Vancouver, would become American and we would gain access to Canada's oil reserves, which made up a large part of their economy. I doubted that Canada would welcome this move and I had reservations about absorbing such a large number of people.

The third area I looked at was Canada's east coast – smaller, but also shared a border with Maine and comprised a small number of Canadian citizens. Less than 2,500,000 people would be affected. It also had a long history of trading with the New England states, and after having been there several times, I began to realize that the terrain and people were more similar to New Englanders than they were many other Canadians.

We of course looked at other interior regions of Canada, while anywhere in Quebec was considered not to be an option. All that talk of separation scared me. I didn't want to buy into a program just to have a key component of the deal go its own way six weeks later.

Ontario was Canada's business community and southern Ontario had far too many citizens; their departure would have had too great an impact on Canadian population numbers. Manitoba and Saskatchewan really didn't have any geographic advantages.

I then asked some of my aides to take a look at these three primary options just for preliminary information, to see if any discussions of this nature were even feasible let alone would get agreement from American and Canadian citizens. In mid-2018 when this committee was formed it had only four members and was of the utmost secrecy. This was a purely hypothetical discussion, and we certainly did not need input from anyone else or any political or global conflict. Fortunately, having small groups of people doing the initial assessments ensured the privacy of the effort.

One thing I learned a long time ago is not to include too many people in the initial stages of theoretical discussions as, inevitably, word will get out. One of the hallmarks of my presidency was to do research before going into a broader process. This is outlined in the "Engaged Democracy" approach. These preliminary discussions gave us the ability to work through many issues on any topic before deciding if it should even become a policy agenda item that we would take to the public.

During Christmas of 2018, I was in Ottawa meeting with the Canadian government over trade issues. We also discussed events in the Middle East and I was working out how to set up educational and health infrastructure there. The Afghan/Iraq/Syrian war had ended a few months before and Canada was spearheading the international infrastructure programs in the area. Along with France, Argentina and Thailand, it was inspiring how the four countries were working together, delivering results in a short period of time.

Paradoxically, the American-led initiatives, in terms of rebuilding the electrical grid and plumbing and highway infrastructure, were a mess. We were working with Brazil, Singapore and South Africa to get this done. The infighting annoyed me and Brazil's president, had to get involved on several occasions to mediate problems. It was a lack of trust from the teams in Singapore and South Africa that affected the operation. Canada did not have this issue as they were trusted implicitly, which is one of the big differences between Canada and the US historically. I was envious of Canada's trusted position in the world and regretted the sense of mistrust that surrounded our nation. It inspired my resolve to change that in the future.

While in Ottawa that December, Justin Trudeau indicated that he would be willing to enter into a private discussion regarding the sale of Canadian land in order for him to reduce his national debt. I'm not sure what he expected me to say and I wondered if he was seriously committed to the notion. He was worried about the reaction of his countrymen should they find out that he was looking to sell off part of the country, and rightly so, I figured. News of this sort could bring down his government. He would need time to figure out what might be the appropriate course of action if this were to happen, and to see what level of funds might be generated. At this point, he was just assessing our interest. Would we do it? I said that I would of course consider it and indicated in a way that inferred I had already given it some effort and that it just might be a feasible idea. He was equally pleased and upset at the same time. I could tell that he was genuinely troubled by what he was suggesting, because as a patriot how do you balance your love of your country and its citizens, with long-term stability and viability. This is a serious ethical issue that many governmental leaders have to face at some point in their term.

On March 2nd, 2019 (my 49th birthday) Justin called me again and suggested that he would at that point like us to seriously consider this proposal. He told me that his government had done a lot of analysis and also polling of citizens to get feedback on what Canada meant to them. They had found out that there would certainly be a financial rationale to proceed. What he also discovered, however, was that Canadians, though unified in support of their nation and its regions, did not seem to hold a genuine concern for their fellow citizens as to whether they were actually part of the country. There were truly distinct geographic and attitudinal divides within Canada.

For example, Prime Minister Trudeau cited statistics that 75% of Western Canadians had never been east of Toronto. Forty percent of Torontonians had never been outside of Ontario. Eighty percent of those in southern Ontario and southern Quebec would rather vacation in the US than in Canada. Maritimers left their home provinces mostly just to get a job elsewhere. It seemed that Canadians had an understanding of what it meant to be a Canadian but did not have a real affiliation with each other beyond their own region. Mr. Trudeau thought that these facts and mindset implied that Canadians who would not be directly affected by a sale would not be overly concerned in what happened elsewhere in the nation and felt that it would not have a substantive affect on the overall fabric of their nation.

His information turned out to be especially true in terms of Eastern Canada. The issue of Quebec separation was a critical one at the time. Canadians had grown quite frustrated that once again this had become a national issue. Therefore, there seemed to be a great deal of animosity towards the Quebecois this time around and more of a willingness to let them go. The three maritime provinces of Nova Scotia, Prince Edward Island and

New Brunswick were generally considered insignificant in terms of politics, business or any other measure of critical influence.

Trudeau was also in favor of minimizing the economic impact of any sale and did not want to affect any large institutions or lose jobs for those involved. He also did not want to create any political unbalance for himself by affecting the number of Liberal seats or unsettle his future voters. He did not want to affect Canada's sovereignty in the northern regions and of course wanted to maintain the bulk of Canada's natural resources for their own future growth. These were all reasonable to me and the committee.

The American delegation indicated that there would not be much to gain from a business perspective by acquiring any part of Canada as markets were generally pretty small by US standards and businesses were unlikely to see much expansion opportunity. Many consumer-oriented businesses were already in Canada like McDonald's, Coke or The Gap so would see little room to benefit from making this into a US territory other than the tax advantages. Depending on the areas purchased there would be offshore benefits by gaining access to Canada's coastal waters, which were abundant with fish and had access to natural gas and oil.

Our second critical finding was that unless a major city was acquired, like Toronto, tax revenue would not be dramatically affected. On the other hand, benefit packages and government assistance would likely go up, so it was recommended to pursue areas of smaller population. Also, there was a cultural aspect of Canada that had to be addressed as there was an acceptance of the US in general by most Canadians, but like a lot of other areas in the world, a distrust of our policies and our objectives was ever present. It was indicated that the area of Canada where this was least significant was in Prince Edward Island, where a feeling had started to emerge that free market conditions were preferred over government regulation.

This was the result of the small size of the PEI market but also the benefits that they had seen once a bridge had been built and connected them with the mainland. When the Confederation Bridge was built, Islanders had direct access to the rest of Canada and their businesses, which were mostly agrarian, thrived. It was inferred that the rest of the Maritime region would feel the same way and that access to bigger markets would encourage them to be more independent. Coupled with access to the larger markets was also the burden of less reliance on government for prosperity.

Take, for example, Nova Scotia. In 2013, 31% of working adults worked for the provincial government and 5% worked for the federal government. 10% were unemployed and received unemployment insurance benefits from the government and another 8% were on social assistance or government retirement pensions. When you added it all up, 54% of the population received at least part of their household income from the government. Therefore, they as a group had become unmotivated and lacked ambition. It was felt that once this reliance on government for subsistence was removed, greater achievements were possible, as the workforce in Nova Scotia was per capita one of the highest-educated areas in the world. From a personal viewpoint, we had found that Nova Scotia had one of the highest rates of university graduates in Canada, so we were quite curious as to why so many of them desired to work for the government?

The final finding by our group was the overall economic decline of the entirety of the region. All the provincial governments were in negative financial positions and services and austerity were becoming the order of the day. The province of New Brunswick was close to declaring bankruptcy. A giant infusion of US dollars, a dollar which at the time was worth around $1.40 in Canada, was extremely attractive.

As a result of our initial discussions, both sides quickly agreed that the area to be considered was to be in the eastern part of Canada bordering on the US, east of the St. Lawrence River and Newfoundland. Montreal was originally not part of the area for consideration. We all agreed that these were our parameters and then Justin and I sat down and outlined some guidelines for the process that we would follow.

The first tenet was that this negotiation would be done in the open and that there would be no initial binding agreement to make a sale of any type by either party. It was agreed that similar negotiations could not be entered with any other country until resolution was reached on our negotiations. We were quite confident that once the world realized that Canada was considering selling part of its territory, a bidding war might begin or that, through the wide reach of politics, the purchase could go elsewhere. We were primarily concerned about the United Kingdom, given its history with eastern Canada. Mr. Trudeau had previously mentioned that he was considering the UK for a similar type proposal, but as yet he had not approached them. We wanted to be in a position of bargaining in good faith, and with trust, so that what we communicated or proposed was not being considered in comparison to on-going negotiations with other parties. It of course was agreeable that if negotiations did not end in a sale, Canada could enter into negotiations with other parties per their sovereign rights.

Secondly, and with much agreement from Mr. Trudeau, we agreed that all policy drafts would be public knowledge and published for input and feedback by the general population of both countries. We would follow my operational "Engaged Democracy" procedures by listening to the fringe, then the moderate experts and finally holding a vote on the issue by informed individuals and the interested electorate. A similar process, though less inclusive, would occur in Canada. They simply did not have the mechanisms to facilitate widespread public discussion at the time.

In Canada, Prime Minister Trudeau wanted to hold a national referendum, and though I was quite opposed to this, I agreed. I was concerned that the lobbyists and interests involved would utilize their financial resources to push through the result that they found most beneficial. My concerns were unfounded – Canadians listened rationally and emotionally to the issues.

Thirdly, negotiations were only to be conducted by an appointed panel of moderates that represented both sides of the equation. Mr. Trudeau and myself were both part of the negotiation teams which was rare, but let's face it, we both had a huge stake in the result of the negotiations in terms of doing the right thing by our respective nations.

Canadians in the affected regions would be given the option to remain as Canadians if they so chose simply by moving west of the St. Lawrence border before the formal handover date of June 1st, 2022. July 4th was the ceremonial date. The Canadian government offered what I considered a rather generous resettlement package of $100,000 per each family plus an additional $50,000 for each child under the age of 18. Canadian citizens would be able to keep their home under the provision that it could only be sold following the hand-over date and to an American citizen.

Mr. Trudeau and I had put forth a lot of research into the attitudes of Canadians and neither of us was too surprised by the time their referendum occurred that only 18% of Canadians affected wanted to remain a part of Canada. A lot of the prior opinion polls had indicated that the rest of Canada did not really have that much of a definitive opinion whether they stayed or left. In fact, many Western Canadians were happy to see a portion of Quebec out of the country. Therefore, not surprisingly, the referendum came back with the result that 62% of Canadians approved eastern Quebec, the Maritimes and Newfoundland leaving Canada. With that ammunition, the affected areas were even more disillusioned with their fellow Canadians and became even happier to leave.

On our side of the border, American citizens, through polling, were tremendously in favor and polling in the most-affected areas (Maine, New Hampshire and Vermont) topped 90% in support. In the rest of the nation, approval of United States expansion rates exceeded 80%. Americans viewed expanded territory as an example of growing US strength. It was also, I feel, a meaningful story for many Americans that the US was capable of geographic growth. The only area that did not register over 80%, but was still in favor of the purchase, was Florida. I guess they were concerned with disrupting the snowbirds that spent so much time in south Florida during the winter months. It turned out to be a non-issue though, as traveling to Florida for these former Canadians became even easier once they were repatriated.

There have been numerous books written on the purchase of the Canadian territories, so I won't go into the details that led to the formal agreement and the handing over of the region. Rather, I'd like to focus more on the results of our expansion and what it meant for us, and for Canada and the rest of the world.

For the US, it showed a tremendous ability to grow our new definition of freedom to a part of the world that was more government controlled than the local citizens themselves even recognized at the time. Once the heavy burden of over taxation, intrusive and over-zealous government regulation and punitive control of daily activities was alleviated, these one-time "have-not" regions of Canada blossomed.

Within twelve months, Kennedy's GDP increased by 24.6%. A result of not only the existing 50 states investing in the area and the military infrastructure we were installing, but also the business acumen of the citizens. As three formerly separate provincial governments were reduced to one for all of Kennedy, many bureaucratic type people found themselves out of work. These people of course had the option to move anywhere in the continental US, but most did not want to leave their homes.

The small business enterprise in Kennedy took off particularly in the health and education fields where private sector investment increased dramatically. These two areas were publicly administered prior to becoming American. However, as part of the agreement, these regions would continue with universal health care for five years, but of course many people understood, as did the insurance companies, that this would be an economic growth bonanza. Insurance companies, hospitals and health care facilities, all opened office after office to compete for business. Likewise, the education sector of America moved into these two regions in droves. Of course, both states had to develop their state bureaucracies and the resultant positive impact on Newfoundland and Kennedy was simply staggering.

Another sector that grew exponentially was the retail sector. Many businesses from New England located to Kennedy and employed thousands of people. One unexpected area where tremendous gains were seen was in real estate. With the American dollar worth more than the Canadian dollar at the time, Canadians in the region exchanged their dollars at par, and as a result their home values sky-rocketed after many people from the rest of the US began to move to the area. People were drawn by the fact that there were significantly less guns and much less violent crime. A very controversial aspect of welcoming these two new states into the union was that they were insistent that their current gun laws remain in effect. These were the first two states where guns were not desired but rather were generally considered illegal and, subsequently, controlled. A unique constitutional amendment was enacted for these two states to exempt them from existing legislation and to abide by their own state court rulings rather than the federal laws.

Newfoundland benefited tremendously from its access to off-shore oil, as well as military installations that were built. Canadian troops that wanted to join the American military were welcome if they could meet US military standards. Those that opted to join the US were immediately reassigned to the area.

The people of Kennedy and Newfoundland saw tremendous individual prosperity as a result of the purchase and to this day have become symbols of the ideal community in the US. They show a commitment to ingenuity through countless web and service industry companies and the growth of the lumber industry. Fisheries have rebounded and are growing exponentially.

Large companies already established in the region were able to maintain all of their holdings but had to make a choice as to whether they wanted to become American corporations or stay in Canada.

This incorporation of Canadian companies into the US was a complex and difficult task. The Canadian system of business is no less complicated than the American when it comes to managing finances and paying taxes. This was a real quagmire for the legal profession, but eventually it was worked out. Canadian-based companies were given the same opportunity as individual citizens to declare their nationality.

However, Canadian businesses would no longer have access to relief once the border was eliminated. The American competitive spirit and federal laws would come immediately into play. The era of government subsidies and protectionism was over for this part of the world.

In Canada, there was of course public controversy over this transaction, but Mr. Trudeau stayed the course amidst significant criticism, including being called a traitor. He explained his position openly and honestly and with the support of the experts he had previously commissioned to prepare the studies he was able to demonstrate, intelligently and confidently, that this plan would work to everyone's benefit. It was difficult to imagine the sell-off of country components, but once you take away the guise of nationalism there wasn't much rationale to resist it. Mr. Trudeau was able to eliminate the national debt and the balance of the country thrived in the new environment and due to the financial surplus that became due to the elimination of transfer payments, Canada now has stronger health care and infrastructure than any country in the world. When Mr. Trudeau eliminated the Goods and Services Tax a couple of years later he was treated like a national hero and ended up winning the largest majority government in the history of Canadian politics in the spring of 2024. The US is now seen as a trusted economic partner and ally for military defense. The fact that we increased our border area with Canada is of no concern. They and we continue to have the longest period of willingness to work together as well and the longest unprotected borders in the world.

As further benefit to the US, from my perspective, is that the goodwill and compassion that the Eastern Canadians had filtered into the balance of New England through migration. New England, already was the most compassionate and open of the US regions and became even more so. Massachusetts previously had a good health care system, and Kennedy now had universal health care for its citizens for at least five years. Part of my wish was that the Governor of Kennedy would then maintain this system at the state level, as I firmly believe in the benefits of universal health care. It may seem hard to believe, but in 2020 there were many Americans who did not agree with this system. Now that basic health care exists for everyone in the US, we have seen an improvement in our overall health standards and length-of-life statistics. Projected for 2050, the average American will live to be 82.9 years, third highest in the world. In 2010, life expectancy was 78.2 years, which ranked 36th globally.

The model that Kennedy created shortly after the merger was a hybrid of the Canadian and American systems, which provided an opportunity to undertake some first-hand democratic experiments.

One thing that became abundantly clear following the purchase of Kennedy and Newfoundland was that there was not a universal approach to certain issues. The great thing about this situation was that it exposed to the rest of America that there may, in fact, be an alternative methodology or approach to what had traditionally been considered etched-in-stone policy. No longer was the cry that something was simply unconstitutional good enough. The one thing that we tried most to hang on to was the "framer's intent" and realized that intent can stay consistent while the implementation can vary.

The quintessential example of the "framer's intent" in Kennedy and Newfoundland was the earlier referenced gun control. I do not in any way shape or form disagree that the

Second amendment gives the right to bear arms. We, however, took a much more rational rather than historical or patriotic approach to reinterpret this right to exclude concealed weapons and all assault weapons.

Handguns and shotguns were allowed but only under license and permit, and maintained existing guidelines on how they should be maintained and when they could be utilized. Of course, in 2020, the usual rhetoric started arose about the rights and freedoms of Americans but with the support of our new American citizens in Kennedy and Newfoundland, who did not want guns in their states, we were able to frame an argument to enforce gun regulation that would not have been possible in any other part of the US. The initial trial period and success of the efforts in Kennedy and Newfoundland eventually led most of the other states to implement similar laws. Today in 2050, only Texas and Alaska have not implemented some form of gun control.

As a result of these gun control discussions, I have been accused on occasion of not defending the Constitution fully, but I disagree with this assessment as the Constitution was always part of any and all discussions. Our argument was based once again on the intent of the founding fathers. It is clear that the right to bear arms is matched with a desire to keep unwanted military personnel out of one's personal premises. This was the result of three guiding objectives in the 1700s. One, the British were to be fought at all costs; two, the right to own property and the subsequent right to protect your private property was something worth fighting for; and three, the freedom to be left alone. Of these three, I clearly think that the second point was the one that the founding fathers were trying to protect. Let's face it, it was the mid-1700s and property was scarce, so the point was that a homeowner who had taken the time to develop and build a property had every right to know that the property could not just be taken away from them and that the use of personal force against any usurper was appropriate. Keep in mind that the new Americans in the 1700s were trying to establish the concept of private property, since they had never had ownership rights while they were in Europe. Also, home owners did not have to acquiesce to any type of governmental expropriation of property. This too was a substantial structural change by Americans, who were unable to resist against the land-owning classes and, in fact, their goods and possessions as well as their private persons were ultimately owned by their superiors while in Europe. These rights would have to be defended by force whenever necessary by the new Americans.

Utilizing this rationale, the case was made that the use of firearms to protect private property was universally justified but limited to handguns. Hunting of course was a prominent part of the culture in Kennedy and Newfoundland and that was not going to change, so shotguns were perfectly acceptable. What were not welcome were concealed weapons and assault weapons, both of which were banned and considered illegal from day one of Kennedy's and Newfoundland's founding. Personal protection on the streets was not considered a valid reason to carry a gun.

Three specific items made this possible.

The first was the willingness of the new US citizens to go along with this approach, and as I mentioned gun control was a mandatory of the new Americans joining the USA. Second was the harsh punishments handed out by the courts towards anyone found with a gun of any sort in their possession without a license or hunting permit. As well, not having your gun secured properly at home or within mobility situations – for example, driving to a campsite – were met with exceptionally large fines.

The third thing was that no costs were attributed to licensing or registering of guns. All guns had to be registered but it was a very easy and non-bureaucratic process. You provided your name, your address, the gun make and model as well as the registration number on the gun. Ammunition did not have to be registered. If you were found with a gun anywhere on your possession or on your property that was unregistered, there was an automatic jail sentence and then a probationary period. If someone used a gun in the commitment of a crime against another then the automatic jail time was a minimum of two years. Discharging a weapon in the commitment of a crime carried with it a minimum sentence of ten years and if an injury was incurred then it went to twenty years. Murder with a gun became an automatic death penalty regardless of what the context was determined to be. If a husband killed his wife, he received a death sentence; if someone killed an innocent bystander, they received a death sentence. Guns were not to be tolerated under any circumstances in the execution of violent crime.

Many at the time considered the automatic death penalty as particularly harsh and inhumane. The death penalty did not even exist in Canada prior to joining the US. The new citizens of Kennedy and Newfoundland though were adamant that the violence that is associated with certain parts of US culture would not come to their states.

As mentioned in Chapter 6, one significant problem with the US legal system in the early 21st century was that all deterrents had been removed from the system. Now, as we know, forgiveness is a big part of the American way but personal responsibility had to become more of an American hallmark. This was especially so in the world of violent crime. For too long perpetrators of violent crime were too often able to escape appropriate justice due to a number of excuses, such as overcrowding of prisons, bureaucracy, inept legal representation, access to superior legal representation and a myriad of other rules that were designed to reflect various socio-economic circumstances etc.

Being considered innocent rather than guilty was a fine moral principle and one that I support fanatically. But once guilt has been established, especially in this instance where we were referring to gun usage, punishment needed to become very severe. The main thing that citizens came to understand was that if guns were utilized in an appropriate manner then no retribution would ever come to that person. However, when guns were utilized in criminal enterprises, then there would be zero tolerance. It only took six months of harsh punishments before the issues surrounding guns virtually vanished over night in the new states. In Kennedy there were only eight murders in the entire calendar year of 2020 and only one involved a gun. In Newfoundland there were no murders and only two incidents of gun violence.

In the aftermath of Kennedy and Newfoundland joining the Union, it soon became clear to most of the other states that gun control could be implemented without a great deal of animosity from citizens and lobby groups. As early as 2019, lobbyists were starting to see their influence dwindle as power was transferring back to the general population. Soon groups like the NRA, though still holding a large voice, were not nearly as influential as in the past, which led to their revised approach towards the safe handling, usage and discharge of firearms.

The weapons manufacturing industry did not fare well under my presidency, and weapons sales have dropped dramatically since. This is consistent with my view of contribution and the concept of wealth-generation. If you make a product that does not benefit a greater good it is unlikely that you will make significant money.

There are of course still plenty of foreign markets where gun sales continue and American manufacturers have been able to exploit those to see growth. I equate gun manufacturing somewhat with the cigarette industry in the late 20th century. Everyone knew cigarettes were bad for your health and people could see there was a drain on society due to health care costs. Over the span of 25 years cigarette smoking fell from 40% to 15%. It became equally clear to Americans that possession of a firearm was not providing any value to their individual lives. There was a famous ad campaign that ran in 2018, claiming that that whenever "Someone sees a gun, someone is hurt." It equated guns with pain and as any psychologist will tell you, most people will do anything to avoid pain.

This great revolution to responsible gun control which originated in Kennedy and Newfoundland took a while to spread throughout the balance of the US, and one can still make an argument that gun control will never happen in Texas.

What happened financially in the new states of Kennedy and Newfoundland was something we had predicted, and the entire government and cabinet took immense pleasure in seeing these new American states succeed.

The irony is that the Maritime Provinces, while in Canada, were labeled as "have not" provinces, and as a result were seen as providing inadequate contribution to the Canadian economy. Over time, Maritimers had come to see themselves as inconsequential both politically and financially. And while there was a healthy small business environment, the main obstacle to success was a lack of access to broader North American markets and high taxation. By eliminating these barriers, and by the citizens embracing a business approach rather than a government-dependent one, the Maritimes thrived.

Politically, the Maritimes had not produced anyone of any political significance to Ottawa since Robert Stanfield in the 1970s.

Upon becoming Americans, and thus becoming involved in the governmental process through "Engaged Democracy" and "3POI-P", the citizens of Kennedy and Newfoundland were able to elevate their political presence through a spirit of inclusion. They had spent so long going unheard that they reveled in the chance to speak out. Since their inclusion in the United States, Kennedy and Newfoundland, due to their unique perspective, have contributed as much, or more, to the national conversation than any other region.

Despite some of the concerns at the time regarding the purchase of Eastern Canada, I knew in my heart that when you remove the blinders of nationalism and create individual opportunity, people will always find a way to overcome and deliver success.

CHAPTER 8

US FOREIGN INTERVENTION... "PROTECT, FREE, ENFORCE"

There was a film, a comedy, in 2004 called *Team America: World Police,* a satirical portrayal of America's military role in the world. I remember thinking it was the funniest of movies at the time, as it was acted by marionettes i.e. puppets rather than actors. Comedy aside, it was also a sober but fairly accurate portrayal of America's self-appointed military role in the world, which all too often left a path of destruction and mistrust behind it. But like it or not, America, since the end of WWII, has been the world's police force. Russia, China and Brazil have all tried to extend a sphere of influence, but the USA still shoulders the responsibility.

After the end of World War II the United Nations was formed, and quickly became an inept body of politicians with no authority or desire to enforce any of its policies. Many parts of the world continued their downward spiral of genocide and attacks against mankind in the 20th century. In recent history, America has had a role in policing the world and this will not change in the immediate future. The dilemma I faced in 2017 was not that the military was ineffective, wasteful or morally bankrupt, rather that worldwide there was a tremendous cynical attitude towards the USA.

Americans were proud of their military and rarely opposed any opportunity to get involved. The rest of the world, however, shared a view that America only enforced its role if there was a national interest to protect or to derive benefit. I vowed to change this view and give our military a broader and more effective role. That role would not only be to defend America and its values and interests around the world, but to be utilized on behalf of citizens that genuinely wanted freedom. Embracing the doctrine of "protect, free, enforce", the American military took on a global political role that people have come to respect now in 2050. America also became a true ally within the realm of NATO and was instrumental in the establishment of an independent global judiciary that gave legal standing to the American military, and its allies, to intercede in foreign countries when enforcement operations were required.

In Iraq and Syria actions taken by the Bush administration against Iraq and Saddam Hussein illustrate how poorly military strategy and tactics were managed 40 years ago. The unilateral US decision to extend military operations into Iraq opened the world up to the growth of Islamic State, which employed terrorist activity as a key element of their operations.

Most of the original IS soldiers were castaways from Hussein's military brigades. They were able to go to Syria and reorganize. Syria was in the midst of a civil war of their own and President Obama was hesitant to get involved.

Hence, through Bush's intervention and Obama's inaction, the US and the rest of the world allowed a new form of military opponent to emerge. Running the military and defending the nation is the most ominous role that the President of the USA has. As an independent citizen, prior to my presidency, I was anti-war, but I could always see when the need for intervention was warranted, if not demanded, for humanitarian reasons.

As President West rather than businessman West, my first goal in the Middle East was to resolve the issues at hand in Syria and Iraq.

Surprising everyone, we pulled out with vows of imposing sanctions and the threat that we would be coming back if any further terrorist activities continued. We were gambling that the alliance forces would be able to handle the job until we returned.

The 2017 pull out was required so that we could pause and develop a position that made sense for the region. Having been there for twelve years already and having seen very few results, we felt that continued military presence without a more tangible goal was foolish and expensive. We knew we would return but we did not see the need to have ground forces.

In truth, we did not do a significant pull out – we just removed the troops from the ground and moved them to surrounding areas where they were asked to stand down until a new plan could be developed. We also suspended our involvement in the bombing missions. We were curious to see how our withdrawal would affect local citizens and government. One of the great threats that kept us in the region since 9/11 was that the area would revert to Taliban control and harbor and foster more and more terrorists. Since the rise of ISIS, there was a fear that the number of terrorists would increase exponentially.

During our withdrawal, we took some military units to Nigeria to put an end to the seemingly unending Boko Haram insurgency, which we put forth as a humanitarian mission and did so without any of our allies or any type of sanction from governmental bodies. We commenced this action using "3POI-P" methodology. I had often wondered if this approach would work in a global environment, one that actually involved life and death, and I was sensitive to the fact that the process takes time, and people's lives are at stake. I also knew that often outside intervention meant the death tolls would be higher than they needed to be.

This level of consideration is the biggest dichotomy that I had to deal with as President. As much as I was in a position of authority, I could not save everybody. On occasion, American involvement might inflict harsh short-term injuries and fatalities in the pursuit of a long-term peace. I had always thought that I had the ability to do the right thing and in a timely manner so that no one got severely hurt. I had held this attitude in a business environment where "not getting hurt" simply meant not losing your job or losing additional benefits. In real life and death situations, though, it was much harder for me to be as thoughtful and as thorough as I needed. It was difficult to accept that one person or group will have to die in order to foster a greater good in the future, a concept that I have never gotten comfortable with and to this day l regret many of the actions I authorized. That is one big part of being President that I do not miss.

In Nigeria, we sent in a medium-sized force, but consisting of all divisions -- Navy, Air Force, Marines and Army – to take out the leadership. Muhammadu Buhari, the President of Nigeria and former general, had defeated deposed president Goodluck Johnathan. Buhari took power in May of 2015 and was much more of a social democrat that his predecessor. He was trying to implement social reforms and welcomed our mission. It took a fair amount of convincing on my part, and I used one of my "trust" cards with President Buhari, seeing that we had worked together during my business career. We had had a tremendous relationship and he knew my personal intentions were honorable. He took a big leap of faith in allowing the US military into the area; the US would not be in the position it is today without his initial trusting gesture.

We needed the chance to prove ourselves that we could conduct an operation without ulterior motives and then follow through on our commitment to leave. To me, this is the essence of policing. Clean up the neighborhood and move on.

Now what happens in your local neighborhood is what happened with Boko Haram. We came into Nigeria with full forces and within ten weeks they were gone from Nigeria and relocated to Chad. There were two repercussions to this. One, we had established that we could conduct an operation successfully by delivering the national government's goals rather than our own. Second, we had foregone the usual rounds of trying to enforce sanctions, freezing funds and negotiating with government through normal channels.

A British peace-keeping force was put in place in Nigeria and given absolute authority in relation to Boko Haram insurgents. They were required to notify the Nigerian leadership of any actions they were going to take. If major skirmishes arose, they were to alert the US, but only then. The entire region was considered a no-war zone and any other country that felt violated by Boko Haram was considered under US protection.

Knowing for once that we could be trusted, the governments of Cameroon, Chad, Niger and Nigeria were able to assemble a coalition military force that combated the Boko Haram insurgency. Just goes to show what can happen when people trust the police.

One of the biggest things I have learned in life, and so many people just don't want to acknowledge this fact, is that there simply are people out there who cannot be reasoned with. These people or groups are going to do whatever they choose regardless of the brutality and consequences for others. These usually have some type of spiritual or intellectual rationale to support their claim to power and you cannot reason with them. Add to this a delusion of invincibility and a fanatic resolve that they will be able to withstand any assault. This type of person can only be dealt with forcibly. Sadly, quite often they take others with them. There have been countless such scenarios since the dawn of humanity.

Once we acknowledged this circumstance in Syria and Iraq, we developed a mandate to remove all of the governing powers while trying to limit a substantial loss of military or governmental life, destruction of property and violations against citizens.

At this point, we could not distinguish any preferred leadership. Syria's president Assad, the leaders of IS and the

President of Iraq, Fuad Masum, had to be replaced. Our intention was that all parties were equally responsible for some aspect of the conflict.

Given our new intention of not intervening beyond policing, we had no desire to remain involved in the political future of the region. Our goal was to quell the violence and then let the chips fall where they may. I equated the situation somewhat to the British withdrawal from India in 1947. I knew there would be massive military clashes after we were gone, but to me, that was the way it had to be. Let the locals fight it out if they must. One of the issues that kept conflict going in the Middle East, was simply the US and western presence. The US and western nations gave the region a common enemy, rather than forcing them to focus on settling their own disputes. If they were enemies, then why were we shouldering the brunt of the opposition?

Until my term as president, there was a general attitude that the US was all-powerful and should determine the direction and course for all nations in the modern world. Now saying that, it is not necessarily untrue; even today we still get involved internationally as much as we can. However, at certain critical points in history you do have to let people resolve their own issues before you can chart a path forward. In the Middle East, the various nations were going to have to come to terms with what type of Islamic culture they wanted. It is foolhardy to try to influence that.

Therefore, after leaving Nigeria in January 2018, we planned of what our role was going to be in Iraq and Syria. We were entering the region with our full military might to remove the leadership of the various groups that were continuing to devastate the region. Our mission would end when Assad and Masum were out of power and IS had been sufficiently destroyed.

It took twenty-two months to accomplish this goal and upon our and the allies complete withdrawal in December 2020, the expected wars commenced. But I am not going to deliver a full history of the events of the Middle Eastern Holy Wars, as there have been a multitude of books written on the topic. The end result however, was that in 2032 the region emerged into the modern world; it was bruised and battered, but had a never-before-seen level of stability and international cooperation.

At this time, unlike in 2017, they also had an unilateral approach to government. It might have been won through force, but at least we knew what form of culture and government we were going to be dealing with.

This view of America as a protectorate met with a lot of opposition initially but ultimately became a valid role and what many hoped would be the primary purpose of the USA military. America had become seen as much more trustworthy and as a result some smaller countries realized they did not have to continue their own military operations and could rely on US intervention if any threat was to arise. Once the fear of war was removed from their country and stability returned to the region then governments were able to focus on building their country's infrastructure and improving the health and education of its citizens. The US would be there to help them if external criminal forces disrupted their efforts. Of course, this required sincere action on our part, as well as not being seen as creating a new colonial system based on a protectorate strong-arm machine. The military protection would come with no price tag attached.

The primary person who assisted in facilitating this global mindset was Justin Trudeau, Prime Minister of Canada. Canada has always enjoyed stability by being essentially a great ally to the USA, but without having to defend its territories as strongly as others do, knowing that America would do so for them. They of course were a good ally and permitted us to utilize their airspace, provided areas for military bases and collaborated on strategic initiatives; yet they remained sovereign and no one other than those trying to gain political advantage ever saw Canada as anything but a free, independent country. Mr. Trudeau went to the UN and put forth the message that America was trustworthy, especially with myself at the helm.

Mr. Trudeau further helped to convince the global community that we were not a violence-prone nation and that compassion and fairness motivated a great deal of our actions. He argued that America was no longer the strong-armed, self-absorbed bully of the world but rather should be seen as a benevolent guiding body of influence that only takes action when grievous violations are being perpetrated. Our motives should not be questioned beyond that. Though I took exception with some of his historical characterizations of our country, I did not intercede, and I felt certain that a third-party endorsement was infinitely more compelling than any words I could use. Yes, perhaps we had to suffer a little indignation, but the end result was my primary concern.

Of course, it took a few years and a few military operations for nations to see the proof and be convinced that we could be trusted.

The premiere example was in Tibet following the events of 2025.

After the death of the Dalai Lama in November of 2024, the new Dalai Lama made the first visit to Tibet since the Chinese government had established strict control 50 years prior. Upon his return, he went directly through the immigration area using his own identification and he was immediately arrested and incarcerated.

Coinciding with Chinese New Year, the citizens took to the streets of Lhasa. Under the guise of celebrating the New Year, the Chinese government, suspecting political insurrection, called for strict order. As the celebrations, over the next week, turned into protests, the Chinese government called for an immediate return to calm in the area. The Tibetan citizens vowed to continue their protests until the Dali Lama was free.

I was watching this situation along with the head of the military. We knew that this was not just a case of removing a political leader; the political ramifications of this project were monstrous. America had good political and economic relations with China in 2025. They were still primarily a communist nation, but in a much more modern context from the 20th century. The Chinese government expected the compliance and obedience of its citizens regardless of their role, position or region. Tibet was considered a Chinese territory and as result the citizens were not entitled to oppose the government or its actions.

To the protesters, the issue was mainly the detainment of the Tibetan Holy Man and that was it. The Dalai Lama had relinquished political authority as far back as August of 2011 when Lobsang Sangay became the Prime Minister of Tibet's government-in-exile. There was very little cry for freedoms or political sovereignty in the rhetoric of the group and there certainly was no political mandate being challenged. There was, however, a growing fear, and it was genuine, that the longer the Tibetan citizens continued their defiance, the more pressure it put on the Chinese government to exercise authority, which would ultimately result in violence. We felt we could step in and manage the situation properly. Our goal of course was to be seen as a trusted partner to both sides, rather than our traditional position of being one-sided and heavy-handed. As this dispute was more about religious freedom and the apparent disrespect being displayed by the government, we felt a negotiated settlement could be reached.

Most people in 2025 considered me foolish for thinking I could mediate the dispute. I will admit that it was neither difficult nor easy, but it required a bout of perseverance, intelligent discussion and a bit of authoritarian attitude to get it down. The main thing to deliver was a collaborative agreement that both sides could feel was successful.

Essentially, all we did was return the system to the status quo whereby the Dalai Lama was a free man but an exile to Tibet, which is the way the situation had been for 50 years. The Tibetan Holy Man though was banished from Tibet and unable to return. The Prime Minister continued to be denied access to Tibet as well.

This resolution was widely criticized back in the USA, with many saying that we did not resolve the situation in Tibet nor did we advance the freedom issue on behalf the Tibetans. Well, one of the most important things I had learned over my 30 years of dealing with foreign governments was that not everyone looks at the world the same way as America does, which is through our own red, white and blue glasses.

In this situation, we came to the conclusion that there was no need to advance any American or philosophical positions; rather, we just needed to resolve the situation without further escalation. The mere threat of military force was enough to have the opponents come to a negotiated settlement. We had the Chinese government come to the conclusion that releasing the Dalai Lama back into society was not a hindrance to their authority over the region. The reality was that they could no longer consider the Dalai Lama a terrorist as they had his predecessor, because he had not done anything tangible with which to be charged. They understood that though he was in favour of independence for Tibet, that he had done very little about it other than write a few essays. The Chinese agreed that an overzealous approach would achieve nothing and that control of Tibet was the primary goal.

The supporters of the Dalai Lama were happy that the Dalai Lama had been released and they saw that symbol as a small sign that they could continue their religious rituals without reprisal of the Chinese government.

The US military had been standing by and fortunately were not utilized other than a small number of peace keepers who entered Lhasa to make sure that no punitive follow-up was ordered by or against the Chinese government. That American forces were allowed into Chinese territory was an extraordinary feat and the first real test of trust and faith and a significant symbol of our warming relations.

At the end of the day our relationship with China was strengthened so much that we started talking about collaborative economic zones for trade. This was huge for the USA, as it opened up the world's largest population to our goods and services and provided even further access to China's manufacturing sector. Keep in mind that the Chinese have had a system of government for thousands of years and just because they attribute a communist banner to their philosophy it does not mean that we should view them as opposition or enemies. They view the world differently than we do, and I have never understood why that bothers Americans so much.

Now saying all that, I do believe in freedom, democracy and the strength of the USA, but the difference in my thinking versus previous Presidents is that I do not think that the spirit of "Manifest Destiny" that infiltrated the American political system throughout the 1850s through the early 21st century is correct for our time. The notion that freedom and democracy should be fostered and promoted by the expansion of USA influence whenever possible is no longer a US government mandate.

The spirit of Manifest Destiny evolved in a different time when there was the desire to expand the natural borders of the USA to the Pacific. In a more balanced world, where the US does not always have the moral and economic position on which to stand, our efforts are better suited towards establishing an open and trustworthy dialogue rather than forcing an agenda.

The USA now has a political system and an economic model that works for just about anyone who wants to embrace it. You can start your own company, get a job, offer your services for hire, sell merchandise, invent something – the opportunities are endless and it has driven our success ever since the first settlers arrived in the New World. Aspects of our economic model have now been embraced by every part of the world able to see how quality of life has improved dramatically wherever capitalism has been implemented. Access to money makes people's lives healthier, smarter and provides citizens with more ability to engage in their personal interests and get involved for the betterment of society as they choose.

The Chinese though, are certainly more geared towards contribution to the state rather than individual gain. Their philosophy, motivated through connection with the world, community orientation, and contribution to a central government, does not inherently make them a group of people to be concerned about. Of course, in our desire to be number one we do not want to see America's standing as the business and economic leader of the world overtaken, so we are rightly concerned that our core beliefs of democracy and freedom should not lose their luster and prominence.

Capitalism can work, as long as everyone has appropriate access to its tenets.

Back at the turn of the century, the reason why many countries started considering Islamic and communist governments was that the American way had become unattractive on many levels. America was still admired in terms of wealth achievement and freedom, but people emerging from totalitarian regimes were not in a position to move to the USA, nor did they have access to sufficient resources and so they chose a political system that, to be blunt, offered the prospect of looking after them rather than having to carve a path of their own.

Following the collapse of any totalitarian regime, governments that offered hospitals, education, food and shelter were the most appealing. Plus, following the government collapse, countries that sincerely came to their aid were also perceived as more favorable. America often would only come to a country's aid of if they could see a tangible national benefit. These were usually the nations that offered military advantage or substantial economic return. With most of the countries in Asia and Africa, this sadly was not the case. We took for granted that any country that was new to democracy would "naturally" choose freedom and democracy over socialism or religious fundamentalism.

What we missed was that nations offering spiritual future were the most welcome. This was especially relevant in terms of religion, and the Islamic nations realized this. When I became President, there was a continued cry in the media against the

Muslim expansion (fueled mostly by ISIS) and there was an outpouring of anger and cries for extermination of the expanding Islamist regimes. Now individual freedom extends to all citizens, and they have the right to choose how they live and what to believe in, yet there was pressure on me to exert military authority over many parts of North Africa and the Middle East as a means of spreading freedom and curtailing Islam. It felt like another Bay of Pigs showdown, but rather than the US and the USSR drawing lines in the sand, it would be the US and the Middle East facing off over the moral strength of Islam versus Christianity. I firmly believe Americans are the "thought leaders" for the modern world. We can use this leadership to take the actions needed to create a world where everyone can exist in a peaceful manner and to pursue their life objectives. But we must choose to be tolerant of other political systems and religious beliefs.

In order to be a "thought leader" for the world, you have to hold genuine respect for these other views. Think about it this way: how often in your life have you done something because someone else forced you too? Probably not too often. If you did end up doing it, you did it begrudgingly and as a result you were likely not as connected with the outcome as you could have been. I always found that if you could get people to do things because they wanted to contribute and feel that they matter, then the results would be substantially better. Once people are motivated you can propose new thoughts and methodologies and philosophies to attain even higher goals.

Now, all that being said, quite often it is advantageous for your counterparts to be fully aware of your seriousness regarding your capabilities and your desires. This does not mean strong-armed approaches to negotiations and conflict resolution, but rather a stated clarity. This all sounds like threatening behavior but utilized correctly it is not. Being number one gives you a distinct advantage.

For example, following the financial collapse of Greece and the attempts by the EU to save it, Greece's internal politics became a shambles and its citizenry was crushed in spirit. Greeks were quite used to prosperity and what I will call a "relaxed work ethic" coupled with extremely generous social policies. When the Greek government could no longer afford to keep up the social policies there was nothing to fall back on and the bottom fell out of their economy. Even at the end and with generous offers from Germany and the EU, there was unwillingness on the part of the Greek population to accept much in the way of austerity measures. Greece declared bankruptcy at the end of 2016.

Throughout 2015 and 2016, already in the midst of austerity, Greece was flooded with refugees from the Syrian civil war. Though many refugees were passing through to other destinations, many stayed, yet Greece could not accommodate the refugees financially, politically or humanely. The circumstances devolved further as refugees started to conflict with the Greek citizens, often due to culture clash. Without international support, no resources and no ability to cope, Greece was further traumatized.

With no where left to turn, in June of 2017 the monarchy of Saudi Arabia arrived with the offer of billions in support. In exchange, they asked for a prominent seat within the future government of Greece. This was not necessarily such a horrific thing on its own, but what was most troubling was that the Saudis were offering direct cash payment and jobs to individual citizens if they converted to Sunni Islam.

Soon mosques were set up as shelter and food areas, such that local Greeks could stop by and get a meal and have a place to sleep if they so choose. At the time, the Saudis were claiming all the assistance was in terms of humanitarian aid and that it was not religious recruitment, but for those on the ground it was obvious what was going on.

Naturally, as economic conditions worsened more people were required to turn to the Saudi supply system and subsequently a conversion to Islam was the only option just in order to survive.

Once again, American resolve was tested; we could not permit Saudi Arabia to gain such control over the birthplace of democracy simply due to economic conditions. If individual Greeks were interested in becoming Muslims that was of no concern, but in this instance this struck the international community more a circumstance of opportunity rather than genuine religious conversion. Obviously we were not thrilled that one of our allies was converting to a potentially Islamic nation. We'd had long-standing diplomatic and military alliances with Greece, and Souda Bay, on the island of Crete, was a major NATO naval base. We did not want to see that slip into another nation's control.

One of the big things I have learned over the years, one I wish more people would embrace, is that before you start to develop and deliver tactics, try to determine exactly what you would like to see happen. I don't consider this the same as goal-setting — to me they are more tangible and concrete measures than to envision what results you would actually like to see.

In this case, our hope was to keep the flow of finances going into Greece to assist Greece in its recovery, to not embarrass the Saudis, but send a message that any attempt to spread religion or to take political advantage of individual citizens would be strongly opposed.

As history has shown, our approach delivered all these results peacefully, and our financial coalition of China, Argentina, France and Russia resulted in Greece's full recovery. The funds were not delivered as aid, but required Greece to open their borders and allow foreign investment. Each of the nations in the plan convinced specific national companies within their own borders to invest substantially in Greece, thus creating billions of investment funds and the resultant boost to the economy. I have never been a proponent of simply delivering aid to a region. I had found through my charitable endeavors and my own business in cash-strapped territories, that the majority of aid doesn't go to those who need it most.

We were able as well to bring Indonesia into the picture to stem the tide of overt Muslim infiltration. Indonesia is the world's most populous Islamic nation and there was a system put in place whereby they were given priority status over the Saudis on Muslim issues in Greece. This way Islam still had input into the development of the mosques and the organization of the formal part of the church in Greece. Their stated goal was to not encourage the spread of Islam, but to assist the integration of individual Muslims into Greek society.

As I have stated, I have no issue with anyone worshipping under any religion as they choose. What I do take issue with, is when individuals, organizations or nations try to spread their beliefs to those who are the most susceptible to receive it. It is not a targeted effort towards Islam, but rather all religions. Looking in the mirror, the USA was guilty of this approach throughout most of the 20th century.

We did, however, feel the need to demonstrate a little muscle to the Saudi navy. We had moved a couple of battleships into the Mediterranean and one aircraft carrier into the Red Sea, just off the coast of Jeddah where the Saudi naval base is head quartered. The NATO allies were also involved in this deployment, giving the appearance of normal training exercises. The intent was not to engage any Saudi naval vehicle, but to demonstrate that any continuation of efforts in Greece would be opening them up to retribution.

Saudi merchant ships could move freely through the Mediterranean, but under the supervision of the Turkish navy, a few Saudi ships were searched without incident. Our navy was in the vicinity whenever these searches were being undertaken but without any direct involvement or even collaboration. The Turkish navy acted in their own manner as they felt warranted.

The message sent to the Saudis was that even though it was orchestrated by the USA, we had full support of the global community and Saudis' actions would no longer be tolerated. The old separation of the world based on political values and lack of trust had finally been overcome; now there would be collaborative efforts to improve the global condition.

On occasion, exterior circumstances also deliver to the result. The events in Greece were overshadowed by the start of the Middle Eastern Holy Wars which distracted Saudi Arabia from mounting any excessive opposition beyond their initial intervention.

Today in 2050, there is now no reason for America to ever start a war of any kind.

I have stated this numerous times and many people consider me a bit soft. I do see the need to maintain a military and I do see the need on occasion to step in to rectify a situation that is out of hand, though we look at that per our normal doctrine of "protect, free, enforce." Today the only reason America would initiate proactive military action would be to counter wars of growth. Whether based on historical territorial disputes, or simply a desire by one country to expand its territory, this will never be tolerated, at least not by military means.

As was initiated with the purchase of Kennedy and Newfoundland, growth can be obtained by mutual negotiation and or legal claims by the newly established global courts of geography. As nationalism has become less and less of a driving force in the world, land transfers have become a more and more common occurrence and have often rectified a situation whereby one region may have invaded the other.

CHAPTER 9

INTERNATIONAL NEIGHBORS AND OPPOSITES...CZECH REPUBLIC AND HUNGARY

My favourite city outside the US is Prague, Czech Republic. It is replete with old world history and as a seat of the former Habsburg Empire it has all the amenities that many cities may not have had built and maintained over time. It has a spectacular cathedral, opera and performance houses, architectural masterpieces, art deco-influenced art and a town square that dates back hundreds of years. The Vltava River dissects the city and the Charles Bridge has been in place since the year 900.

President Obama held his first international rally in Prague and I staged two public addresses there during my term, the first in June of 2017 when I addressed American international foreign policy and outlined USA objectives for all of Europe. This was my first public address conducted outside of the continental USA and it placed me in the a global spotlight for the first time. When President Obama had his Campaign of Hope in 2007, his presence in Prague made him into a world-notable person. At one point earlier in my life I had lived in Prague for six months and even considered moving there. It is a fantastic city, a unique blend of history, culture, art and politics in a country that has wonderful people who, in our lifetime, have struggled for freedom, been shut down by the Russians, been accepting of their persecution, fought back a second time, won their freedom and then struggled with becoming a democratic nation. It makes for very interesting conversations.

Further, the Czechs were the first to brew pilsner ale in a town called Plzn, and anyone who knows me at all is aware that my favorite beer in the world is from Czech Republic and is called Pilsner Urquell.

Prague is a unique blend of freedom and hesitancy. Czechoslovakia had a forced membership in the USSR after WWII. I think it is fair to say that the people of Czechoslovakia were not really supporters of the communist notion and were simply delivered into Stalin's hands by the allies after the war. Though there was indeed some socialist thinking in the area at the time, the citizens were in fact proponents of freedom and admired the western world. They were greatly disillusioned following WWII, feeling the western allies had abandoned them following the Paris Peace Conference.

There was a movement towards freedom in the late 1960s, one that gained real traction both on the ground and within the Czechoslovakian government. However, the "Prague Spring" movement was quashed when the Russians rolled tanks into Wenceslas Square in August of 1968. The government, wishing to avert a greater tragedy for the Czech people, reaffirmed control with the local communists, who then worked with the Russians to persecute and impugn those responsible for the movement. To this day these officials, now long dead, are considered traitors to the Czech Republic, but under the circumstances, and without any real military strength or western military support, they really did not have much of a choice.

Through the 1970s the freedom movement was pushed so far underground that most citizens did not feel that they had any hope of freedom. They simply had to recognize the fact that their country was being controlled by the Russians and resign themselves to this circumstance.

Citizens were forced to show up for great state holidays and pageants, and the secret police could persecute anyone believed to be against the party. Many Czech citizens were forced to betray friends and family or face persecution at the hands of the communist party.

This era of persecution by one's neighbors is still evident in today's Czech Republic, as no one seems to trust each other there. Very little of substance is ever put in writing and no one ever says "no," which was forbidden under the Russians. Therefore, silence is an appropriate response of disapproval.

I found the Czech mindset to be one of the most interesting in the world in the late 20th century. For example, take the typical 50-year-old at the time. They were born into the communist regime in 1950. They were in all probability at the age of 19 one of the protesters fighting for freedom in 1969. They would have been forced back into communism under the threat of death or imprisonment after having tasted just the basic elements of freedom, such as freedom of speech and freedom of assembly.

Then through the 70s and early 80s you followed along with the strong-armed police and did as you were told. You relinquished all your claims on freedom, ambition, hope and quite simply became a drone. Intelligent aspects of your mind were turned off as they were considered a threat to the state. You essentially tended to your family and did what the party told you to do without question.

Then in 1989, at the age of 39, you suddenly were free to do what you wanted. You could get any job, do anything you chose, say anything you chose, you did not have to be scared of the police and there was a politician in Vaclav Havel, a humanist leading the country. This is the first time in your life that you have been able to express any of these feelings or thoughts. How would you go about it? You are in the prime of your life. This question I find eminently interesting and I doubt I will ever know what I would have done under similar circumstances.

The reality of what happened in the days following the Velvet Revolution which swept through eastern Europe, was that foreign investment did most of the profiteering. There was a crime wave of epic proportions, corrupt government officials raided coiffures, the university-educated class (mostly the younger people) got all the good jobs and the average 39-year-old man I just described got virtually nothing in the immediate aftermath of the birth of freedom. After a few years of euphoria and economic improvements which benefited almost everyone, there was a distinct contrast between the foreign owners, the educated locals, and the long-suffering citizen who had done most of the politicking and on two separate occasions stood up for freedom.

As a result, disillusionment crept back into the system after about 15 years and by the early 21st century some saw the communist party as a genuine option for the future of the Czech Republic.

In neighboring Hungary, for example, which had followed a similar history, extreme right-wing politics returned and the politics of hatred resurfaced and ultimately lead to war. In Czech Republic though, people are more freedom-loving and have spent much more time trying to improve a system that is fundamentally broke, surprisingly even more so than the American government was broke at the time.

To me, Czech Republic represents one of the finest examples of commitment for freedom. There was opposition at all times but never violence against the Leninists, the Nazis, the Stalinists or the Russians. Czechs have often been accused of being weak, unable to resist the occupation of their territories by foreign nationals, but I feel it served them better over the long-term than many of the nations that resisted and ultimately had their cities destroyed and citizens murdered in the millions. For Czechs, freedom was a struggle the lasted over 100 years and saw three different groups occupy the region, and then they had to suffer the indignity of the allies selling them out to Hitler and then

Russia. That they endured this demonstrates a tenacity and perseverance that I feel only Americans have been able to match. In 2019 I took on a unique role that allowed me to partner with the Czech Republic as an official in their governmental process where we started to implement reforms and practices that had been so instrumental in the growth of the USA.

In 2018, it was considered lunacy that the government of the Czech Republic had to face a non-confidence vote in their parliament. Fortunately, my affinity for the area and the fact that I had lived there allowed me to partner with Bohuslav Sobotka, the Prime Minister, in an all out effort to keep him in power. It took a lot of hard work but the basic message that was put to the Czech citizens was that the biggest organizations in the world were with you.

This was the first time that the spirit of "constructive capitalism" took an international leadership and collaborative mindset. Governments, companies and organizations (foreign and local) would start to band together to improve the overall well-being of the specific suffering nation.

I used to make a comparison at the time, stating that all the biggest organizations in the world have a Board of Directors from outside the company, so why could a nation not accept positive influence from outside nations. This was not an attempt to usurp the sovereignty of Czech Republic, but a genuine effort to improve their economic and social conditions. Once again, I think that the trust and the cooperative nature that I had developed not only in Europe but around the world allowed me to take this risk and to enter into this arrangement with the government. The fact that I got to visit the Czech Republic twice a year was a nice personal bonus.

The concept of an outside federal management group (OFMG) working with federal local politicians is now a universal concept in 2050. The intent is always to bring efficiency to government, develop the economic platforms of the nation and to ensure a benevolent and honest government from the members that are in charge.

In the Czech Republic, America, along with other foreign service, were able to work with the Czech Republic's government to institute a health care system, educational structure, electrical capabilities and a capitalist model that reflected their own wants and desires.

One of the dilemmas that emerging nations often faced was that private foreign investment usually steam-rolled local interests and ownership ultimately landed in the hands of outsiders. With the OFMG approach, this was avoided from day one as national governments understood the issues that needed to be addressed and were able to institute them and regulate foreigners to the betterment of the local citizens.

Numerous countries in North Africa benefited greatly from OFMG during the later period of the African Spring, whereby citizens were still rebelling against authoritarian rule that had existed for 50 years. There, countries such as Tunisia were able to reach a measure of independence and democracy as early as 2012. However, while they achieved great success other nations such as Egypt and Libya did not know what to do once they ousted their government. The simple truth was, they just did not understand democracy and the modern economy.

Finally, in 2021, in Egypt, they called upon the British to assist them in establishing democratic principles that suited their unique part of the world and were subsequently able to establish a suitable form of democracy. The British were not called upon to exert military force, only to utilize their skills at developing a democratic process.

The really impressive thing about democracy is the flexibility of it.

The Egyptian government by the year 2022 instituted a Republican process but had a set of rules regarding who could be part of the Cabinet. For the first time, all high-ranking political appointments had to be voted upon. This was an unique blend of the British parliamentary system whereby all members of the Cabinet come from the Elected House of Representatives. However, the Prime Minister, who is the head of the party that wins the election, got to appoint them.

In the Egyptian model, not only is the President an elected official, but so are all the Cabinet members. Therefore, the party system is completely meaningless and those candidates running for the elected positions have to run dual campaigns. One, to be elected as a member for their own constituency, and the other to be a member of the Cabinet. It is not a rarity that a member of the House of Representatives is a member of Cabinet yet is not a voting member of the House. This is a tremendously unique situation anywhere in the world and one that many other nations are looking at.

The nice thing about democracy is that it can take any form that the people want. In the USA's model of "Engaged Democracy" the people have the maximum input possible. Many people pushed me to make the model global, but I always state the same thing: "The world is a varied place, and though our logic and thinking are at the forefront of freedom and democracy, other parts of the world have different systems and histories. Therefore, they cannot just embrace our models over night." The goal of OFMG is always to bring the right type of democracy, and then allow the evolution to continue naturally. This is the learning of history.

The best thing about the OFMG initiative is that no time had to be wasted with trial and error for programs. Best practices existed everywhere in the world for all aspects of economic and social programs as well as how to fund them. Expertise in these areas was widely shared by the foreign services of just about every nation in the world. At the onset of the program, we had 42 countries willing to participate and to provide counsel through their diplomatic services. This was a monumental breakthrough in the era of political detente as governments actually grasped the concept that by allowing use of their nationals to assist in the development of other parts of the world, it would create a better world in general.

The biggest structural difference regarding our modern operating model and the one which constituted organization like the United Nations, the International Monetary Fund and the World Bank, was that these old groups all served too many masters and had to try to balance and weigh interests of all its member organizations. With the "Outside Federal Management Group", the mandate was much more single-focused and subsequently secondary interests were not as prominent in the day-to-day focus of the committees. This focus of the OFMG resulted in reforms moving at unprecedented speed, as well as a consistency of objectives across common regions. For example, in Laos in 2032, economic stability was provided by a state-managed central banking model and local and international trade guidelines were established. Citizens were all provided with communication tools and internet access through either PC's, smart phones or internet cafes. Tax systems were established as well as education systems. OFMG however was not to be involved in instituting any specific type of governmental system. Democratic institutions were to evolve naturally. Any area that wanted to, could abandon their local currency and had the choice of joining one of the trade areas that had been established and switching to the currency of that zone.

As with Europe, trade areas became much more relevant for the ease of economic development and the desire to create a more stable global trading platform. When the world ended up with only seven major currencies and trading areas in 2025, that eliminated a great number of discrepancies and also created multiple trading areas and broke down petty barriers and restrictions on freedom of trade.

The currencies are the same as we know them in 2050. The Dollar in North America, the Euro in all of Europe, the Yan in

Asia, the Yen in Japan, the Australian dollar, the Brazilian dollar in South America and the Pound in the UK and Africa. There are still some countries that have kept their own currencies, but the International Monetary Fund is working with those governments to convert to their regional standard as a means of seeing improvements and genuine stability.

On the other side of the international diplomacy scale was Czech Republic's neighbor, Hungary.

In 2022, the world was on the brink of war as Hungary retreated into the old European ways that they and the rest of the world had found quite deplorable. Based on the politics of exclusion and persecution, insular policies, controlling dictatorial central control and even xenophobic activities, the Jobbik movement had been swept into power four years prior on a campaign based on reforming immigration law, standardized education, strict governmental centralized economic planning, enforcement of law and order through police strong-arm tactics and a spirit of retribution against the governments and elites of past governments and business. This all sounded quite familiar to many people at the time, and the alerts had gone up all over Europe.

Prior to the Jobbik election in 2018, the red flags had tacitly gone up, but when a right-wing party gets swept into power anywhere, especially in central or east Europe, it is alarming given the history of the region. To be blunt, the Jobbik government certainly had some of the hallmarks of neo-fascism and were implementing some of the same tactics through the advent of the black-shirted street police -- aka the Hungarian Guard – who would enforce compliance and on occasion attack dissidents. Further, there was a substantial increase in the detainment of political opponents which led to on overall decrease in political debate. What little debate that did continue was mostly from underground groups. The Hungarian Parliament had become devoid of political policy-making and free discussion.

As I mentioned, the Czech Republic was a freedom-loving and forward moving society. Hungary certainly had not followed the same path after the Velvet Revolution of 1989. As a result, they had not received as many of the same benefits. The Czech Republic eventually became a prime example of a modern capitalist model based on capitalism, freedom and democracy. Hungary had never been able to move to that point. Corruption had never been eliminated from the Hungarian's government's operational system.

The second issue was that the government had kept a primary role in central economic planning so foreign investment and an entrepreneurial class of locals did not materialize the same way that they had in other countries. The union movement continued to be strong in most parts of Hungary but other than for a few local business people in Budapest, few citizens saw significant gains as a result of the end of Russian occupation. Even those who did achieve great wealth received it due to the grace of the government through contracts and select handouts and appointments. In many instances, there seemed to be an overt padding of pockets through contracts that required virtually no work in return. Very little effort was actually made by the government to hide this condition. Kickbacks were common and to most of the Hungarian citizens it was widely-known that to get a local contract a payment of some sort was required to the local magistrates.

Essentially what happened in Hungary from 1989 onwards was that the social and political systems stagnated or regressed. Other than a few infrastructure upgrades in housing, electricity and roads, the average Hungarian saw extremely little difference. In fact, Hungarians might have claimed that times had been better prior to 1989, as they were treated much more humanely and fairly by the Russians than they were by their own government. Young people began to leave the country as soon as they were done with school, leading to an exodus of talent. They knew there were few professional positions other than in engineering or government and even jobs in these areas were limited to parties who had existing government or economic connections.

At the time, the Russians were suspected of supporting the Hungarian government, but I did not see any intelligence to support this claim. Russia had enough issues to deal with and was not all that interested in reassembling the USSR, as some Americans may have thought. Further, Russia had formally annexed the Crimean by this time and the international community was opposed to any further expansion.

Further, the Hungarians certainly did not want the Russians back in their country. It was clear as well that the Hungarians were not all that interested in listening to any other foreign interest and wanted complete control over their future. Unlike those in Czech Republic, who had welcomed the OFMG, which was able to provide advice and expedite improvements and integration with the global community, Hungary chose to go it alone and subsequently started leaning towards a dictatorial and insular approach.

I first met with Hungarian President Barreh Trük in 2018 about five months after the Jobbik party had come to power. He had a belligerence and intolerance that seemed out of control and approached our conversation with an over-protectiveness and hesitancy that any old world chiefs of cold war era would have been proud of.

The Hungarian President, I could tell, wanted to control the conversation and the line of discussion.

The argument articulated by President Trük was that I could not possibly know the situation in his area as well as he did, therefore everything I said or did would be considered inconsequential. An attitude of this nature rarely leads anywhere positive, but I have known a few businessmen who are obstinate enough to not listen to anyone and have produced significant accomplishments, so I did not dismiss Trük and I thought that, as I now knew more about him, discussions might still go well since I could change my tact.

However, in early 2019 the Hungarian army violently put down a demonstration against a new insurance program. The government had decided that every Hungarian citizen who was already entitled to full health care coverage should now contribute more to receive this benefit. For context, Hungary was already one of the most highly-taxed areas in Europe and this increase in insurance premiums was not well-received by people who barely made enough to survive and had to rely occasionally on bread rations and milk.

When a scandal broke that several high ranking government officials, including the President, were pilfering funds directly from road-toll taxes that were collected at just about every entry/exit on Hungarian highways, the local citizens became indignant -- they were being asked to pay new insurance taxes while their existing taxes were being stolen by those in government? The government responded by launching an inquiry but after two months the inquiry reported that there had been no wrong-doing. The *Magyar Times* conducted a thorough examination of the same program and discovered documents that implicated at least six members of the government. There was no direct evidence against President Trük, but it was widely acknowledged that he was complicit in the misdirection of funds and had received gain from them.

When the street protests started on February 12th, 2019, over 10,000 people assembled at Heroes' Square in the heart of Budapest. On the first day, it was relatively orderly. The next day, however, over 50,000 citizens showed up, damaging property, burning piles of trash in the square and instigating several violent confrontations with the police leading to dozens of arrests.

That evening the government's response escalated. By midnight, the militia had been deployed and by three o'clock the crowd was surrounded. When the crackdown started, the police led the initial foray with tear gas, intended to disperse the crowd, but after fifteen minutes the army and armored vehicles moved into the middle of the Square and any person that came within arm's length of a soldier was detained, quite often violently. Fifteen minutes later the soldiers took a more direct assault on those that had remained (some 25,000). Within minutes the military was in complete control of the entirety of downtown Budapest and the uprising was over. When the sun came up on Valentine's morning, over 400 people had been killed. When I heard the news I telephoned President Trük. He surprisingly took my call, and strongly indicated that my intervention was not desired. He further stated that the issue at hand was simply "a matter of Hungarian national security, and that as a free and independent state it was entitled to operate as it deemed suitable." I reminded him that the use of force by any government against unarmed citizens is never permissible, and that the acts of his government and army were inexcusable and could not under any circumstance be condoned. He countered that this was an action of stability and peace-keeping in his own nation and iterated that the media were prone to exaggerate the circumstances, and he assured me that no private citizen had been unnecessarily killed in the action and any that fatalities were the result of self-defense measures. He assured me that I would have followed the exact same procedures. I disagreed with him on that point, and after a few more minutes of essentially barking at each other we ended the conversation. President Trük and I would never speak again.

To me, the worst thing any leader in any country can do is take the life of its citizens. This is the ultimate violation of freedom and is the antithesis of what government should do.

The number one purpose of any government is to protect and to serve the citizens of the country. This is the foundation of modern government in the mid-21st century. Any government official who would condone the use of mortal force against its own citizens is not ruling in the right mindset and ultimately should not be in any position of authority.

The hallmark of "old world governmental authority," be it democratic, monarchist, communist or shogun, was that individual citizens were considered expendable for the greater good of the state. Whether the disregard was through military action, genocide, political manoeuvring or indifference, the era of death by governmental decree was coming to an end, and a new mantra was coming into place. America had long been a preacher of freedom and liberty but had many notions such as "freedom is not free" and idioms of that ilk. Concepts like this led to the conclusion that human life is a cost of freedom. I disagree vehemently.

This notion may have been true in the 20th century when that era endured two world wars and fighting for land and political gain was the system still most prevalent in Europe. However, especially after the First World War, most individuals came to realize that wars of this nature were simply not sustainable nor beneficial to anyone. The devastation done to the human and physical world exacted too high a toll with millions of dead, destroyed cities and environments.

It had become clear to the civilized world by the turn of the century that use of individual citizens as pawns in the pursuit of national interests was not to be tolerated. It was acknowledged that each nation required a military for defense and potentially for world peace-keeping efforts. However, these militaries were to be voluntary and internationally focused. In 2050 it is almost inconceivable in the west that an army would be used against its own citizens.

The fact that President Trük would order force against his citizens and then defend the action, meant that he was not capable of ruling in a benevolent manner and would be capable of any atrocity against the world. If a leader is willing to kill his own citizens, then it is highly probable that he would take action against foreign lands and people. President Trük's actions over the years pushed the world's and the American military to consider taking action.

Following the Hero's Square massacre, President Trük created a special, independent police force.

Initially, there were no serious problems as the new force kept themselves to the same type of issues that the local police force would have gotten involved in, but the fact remains that in any situation that was considered uncertain, this new national force usurped local police jurisdiction. Initially the new force contributed significantly to decreasing street crimes, running brothels out of business and controlling public intoxication. It was difficult to complain too much. It wasn't until six months later that they started exerting a far-reaching role in the future of Hungary.

The first case of this was in a town called Herend where the state police forced a porcelain factory to change its management and put in place party members of the Jobbik. This was met with a demonstrable outcry from the local employees and of course the company management and local government who were part owners in the venture. The new managers were given the shares and profitable aspects of the previous group. Two of the managers who were specifically vocal in their outrage against the Jobbik government were subsequently thrown in jail. There had been a public trial, but it was so poorly run, and the sentences were too easily arrived at that even to the state it could not appear to have been a fair trial. In hindsight, Trük wanted to test the local citizens to see if he could get away with these types of actions. In his memoir, he does, in fact, hint that this was the case. He also claimed that it was a move that rewarded some of his boyhood friends for their loyalty to him and that there shouldn't have been any protest at all, as this was a legitimate move that happens all the time and in every part of the world.

One smart thing that Trük did, was to ensure that no employee or local citizen was harmed in any way either physically or financially. All the employees at the porcelain factory were retained and within six months another fifteen workers had been hired from the local population due to the tremendous results brought forward by the new management. These business results were never proven to be true or false, and most people suspected it as a PR move to show that the new management was better than the ousted group. The intent was that the residents of Herend be the ones to benefit the most. It worked with immeasurable success.

After the two original managers were put in jail for terms of three years each, and the new employees were hired, after six months no one openly said too much about it. Even the local paper expressed approval with the new management (which was later exposed, in documentation, following the fall of Trük, to be the result of a major increase in ad sales to the newspaper by government and state-owned businesses).

At the same time, Trük had started building his troops in Hungary, and there were many reports from the area of increased military spending and manufacturing. The army in Hungary grew dramatically, from 250,000 in 2008 to nearly a million by 2018. National military service for every Hungarian male once they turned seventeen became mandatory in 2017. At this time, there was no real evidence that Hungary had any designs on waging war with anyone and there was no indication that they were going to turn to Russia for support. Though there were remnants of the old Soviet and German empires in the region, and some still called out for a return to communism, the thinking was that Hungary was growing in strength and wanted to exercise more authority. They were additionally looking to exercise a bit of muscle in order to take on a much more aggressive position in terms of their political situation and to perhaps even shore up a bit of their national defenses as a result of the growing western collaboration with the Czech Republic and a criminalization to the east that continued in Ukraine. These were both reasonable assumptions and were affirmed by President Trük as legitimate and sovereign reasons for growing military might. We were closely monitoring the events in Hungary, but were not yet moved to action.

Following the Treaty of Trianon at the end of WWI in 1920, Hungary had its borders substantially reduced. Many natural-born Hungarian citizens were forced to live outside what were then the new Hungarian borders. One area that was lost under that agreement was Transylvania, which had been ceded to Romania in 1920. During WWII, Hungary entered Transylvania and, with the support of the Nazi's and Mussolini, reclaimed the region. They were once again forced out by the Treaty of Paris in 1947. Hungary was at one time part of the Austrio-Hungarian Empire and was a seat of power and authority under the Hapsburg Dynasty in Europe. With historical blinders on, Hungary still clung to a vision of glory and power that had been once seen as the scourge of Europe.

It was known that President Trük had approached the President of Romania on several occasions to try to negotiate what he considered a repatriation of native Hungarian lands to their rightful nation. The negotiations never progressed.

With that history in mind, on July 17, 2021, 200,000 Romanian citizens living in Oradea, just 12 kms from the border with Hungary in northwest Romania, were awakened by the Hungarian ground forces as they rolled into their town. There were no guns fired, no artillery blasts, and no bombs bursting. Everyone was caught off guard and no one in the Oradea region could mount a resistance in such short time, so the Hungarians took over. The Hungarian army parked a couple of tanks on Republican Street and at a few other landmarks like the Baroque Palace. They went to the local public house and barred the mayor and the council from entering. Amazingly, there was not one fatality, and only a couple of minor injuries in the four hours it took to move the troops and military into the city. By two o'clock in the afternoon the Hungarians had raised their flag over the government house in the city.

What shocked the world even more, was that no one even heard of this until six weeks later, when a Romanian citizen from the region wrote a letter to the editor in a Bucharest paper wondering if the Romanian government was going to take any action or whether Oradea was now part of Hungary again. Now, I couldn't really call it an invasion as it didn't feel like one. Ultimately, the citizens in Oradea, who were mostly Hungarian descendants, were happy to be again part of a country where they spoke and language and had a common heritage. The Romanian citizens in the area were treated well by the Hungarian forces and, in fact, the citizens of the town were given great amounts of cash and jobs that derived from the military presence in the area. Soldiers were housed and fed by local establishments and jobs were created with the construction of a military establishment on the outskirts of the town. Everyone seemed to be gaining from this, which was the same approach that Trük had implemented in Herend, just on a larger scale. Remove the existing leadership put in economic gains for those that normally should have held opposition to the events, and find a means of quieting protesters. This last item was not an issue as the mayor and council of Oradea were given vast sums of money as well as high-ranking positions within the Hungarian political structure in Budapest. The president of Romania shockingly claimed that he did not know of this action either, which makes you wonder how much money went into his pockets.

Once word finally got out, the United Nations convened and prepared one of their non-substantive documents. America, however, had a different stake in what had happened there. The Czech Republic had been an exemplary role model of modern world collaboration and saw tremendous economic success and cultural stability as a result. With the Czech Republic being so close to the borders with Hungary, I was worried. How might it affect Czech growth? I was also concerned with the international legality of the situation.

Finally, I was worried what Trük might be planning as a next step in his military advancement. It should have been a non-issue, since any military action based on aggression or acquisition was considered an immediate violation of international law and a policing unit, under the auspices of the American military model, would enter the region and return stability through force and negotiations.

In this instance, though, there was history and there did not appear to be any aggressive action though acquisition definitely had occurred. Also, the locals did not mind the Hungarian forces being in their city. The question at the time was, does an invitation need to be sent out for an action to be acceptable?

To me the answer was an unequivocal yes. A foreign military had crossed into another nation's territory, and whether there had been force or not was inconsequential. Historical context had no bearing on the situation. What did have influence, though, was the response of the citizens of Oradea.

The doctrine we had defined for our military – *"defend, free, protect"* – did not seem to apply in this situation, so it created a quandary. The Jobbik party, though not entitled to be there, were welcomed, so one could make the argument that they were liberators in terms of freeing Hungarian citizens from Romanian territory. However, the issue was, could territory be reclaimed if the citizens wanted it?

The thinking we developed was that if the citizens of Oradea had invited the Hungarian army into their area then there was no real reason to vehemently contest the action. But if the army had made the initial foray then that movement had to be addressed.

We must remember, the concept of nationalism was starting to dwindle, especially in this part of the world. Central and Eastern Europe had been carved up repeatedly over history, and had become a patchwork of nations that often had very little history or communication with the nation that they were currently part of.

For example, utilizing my best-case scenario of the Czech Republic, they did not exist as a nation unquestionably until 1992. Prior to that it was a group of disparate regions, mostly Bohemia and Moravia, which had been a member of one alliance or another throughout its history. Only in 1918 did it become recognized as Czechoslovakia as part of a democratic union with Slovakia. It was controlled by Nazi Germany and then the USSR. Even after the Velvet Revolution it took another three years for it and Slovakia to become independent nations.

The bottom line was that this region had no sense of continuity in terms of nationalism, people, politics or geography. Therefore, as part of a group with the United Nations, we determined that the military action carried out by Hungary may not be as one-dimensional as we initially thought. I continued to argue that the Jobbik party needed to be stopped in its expansion efforts, believing they planned to continue to repatriate historical lands. I also, however, was willing to tolerate that the Jobbik party could stay in power given my view of a nation's right to self-determination.

What we decided to do, surprising the world, was allow Oradea to remain as part of Hungarian territory, but the act would retroactively be treated as a purchase. Though the Romanian government was initially against this approach, the amount of funds that was being discussed was extremely large. Not surprisingly, they acquiesced. As land swaps were becoming more and more common, there was not much need to take a military route, but we wanted to make sure that the world got the message: there would be significant cost if actions of this nature were attempted in the future.

In this instance, as a means of ensuring that further land forays were not going to happen under any circumstances, the Chinese army placed its soldiers at the Cluj-Napoca military base just north of Oradea. They were tasked with monitoring the

Hungarians, who had to withdraw their military vehicles from Oradea.

The next thing we insisted upon, was that the Jobbik government accept OFMG.

As mentioned, the Jobbik party was not necessarily embracing the principles of freedom and democracy and had exacerbated their position by adopting some politics of intolerance. With humane theories of government becoming the appropriate ones, we wanted to give them access to greater thinking and expertise.

Of course, the Jobbik government was opposed to this. They felt the financial remuneration was sufficient. In my mind, we could not acquiesce – it would give the Jobbik credibility for their actions. Basically they would have just paid a financial penalty and got what they wanted.

Given the coming Chinese presence, the Hungarian government, in a move to try to be political, insisted that an Asian presence be the key contributor on the OFMG panel. In their minds, this situation would provide an east vs. west circumstance and they could operate while the two foreign factions went head-to-head on issues. Smartly, the UN group selected Singapore as their OFMG partner. The partnership worked fantastically.

What the Hungarians had failed to recognize was the spirit of conflict that had so permeated east vs. west relations for so long had now evaporated. The world was globalizing. Though there may still be some political and philosophical opposition, there was none anymore when it came to practical matters of finance, war or humanity. The world had moved away from the destructive forces of opposition and could see the benefits to collaboration for a greater good.

Let's face it, China was growing exponentially year after year, and the prospect of opposing the western world was one that they had come to realize was not to their benefit. Their economy reaped the benefits and, due to the creation of the Yan as the pan-Asian currency, their global position was second only to the US.

The Hungarian movement died and few in the world today remember that the Oradea occupation even happened. It turned out to be just a small event but given former approaches i.e. American military intervention, it could have easily escalated into a major war.

Back in 2016, most governments' foreign service, including the USA's, existed to serve the needs and protect the interests of the country they represented. For example, in 2016 the US had over 10,000 people working in the Foreign Service and over 6,000 of them were posted overseas. These people did one of two things: administer to the requirements of American citizens that were in these countries and develop partnerships in the various sectors of the local economic and political environment fostering American business and political interests in the area.

As the Outside Federal Management Group (OFMG) concept flourished, we felt it necessary that the US foreign service provide greater resources to American business as a means of gaining a competitive advantage internationally.

We looked inwardly at the role of the Foreign Service with a new goal in mind. We of course were in no way going to tamper with anything affecting role number one. Servicing and looking after American citizens overseas will always be the primary task of the embassies and consulates wherever they are. We did look to minimize the role that number two played and tried to get our foreign service more involved in the development of the local economy and political structure, so that they fit into their regional economic trading area. This way we had a better understanding of what we were dealing with on a regional scale.

The Foreign Service would also establish relations with local governments and the international community, such that social and cultural programs could be exchanged.

Penultimately, appeasing issues of racism and prejudice were part of their new role and the hope was that previously-held beliefs that were detrimental to individual freedoms in terms of gender, religion, and ethnicity were eradicated in the ways and means of government, a goal we are getting closer and closer to each day.

Lastly, we toned down the scope of the CIA's collection and monitoring of foreign governments. The CIA was focused more into the area of identifying threats to American soil and overseas threats to business and personal issues. Also, we increased the CIA's role in collecting information on criminal activities. Though it is necessary to monitor some foreign powers the new global-interconnectivity has become the great deterrent – everyone has such a huge stake and benefit to the process working properly, that no government would ever risk an attack to it.

An expanded role of the America foreign department is to be a business consultant for American companies operating overseas. Though American businesses were slow to warm to the new role, over time it turned out to be invaluable, giving American business a step up when entering new areas. The business branch of the foreign governmental service provided services, from market information to partnership identification, governmental contact information, taxation advice, and cultural assimilation. The program, though managed by Americans, was generally operated and implemented by locals.

When we first developed this concept it was scoffed at. There was a lack of willingness by locals to work with the US government as well as the fear of attacks on American targets due to the nature of the program, which required businesses and perhaps governments to disclose sensitive information. These were issues we took into consideration and we decided that only one goal needed to be addressed: the requirement of mutual trust.

As this was primarily a government service to the business community, the first place we turned to was American business. Top business leaders were stunned when we contacted them for advice and I think there was an element of distrust that we were trying to meddle into their businesses.

The big difference from the past was that we indicated to all businesses that we were developing a service, but there would be no obligation for businesses to utilize the service and there would be no cost other than a bit of consultation in the set-up days if they wished. Under these guidelines half of the companies we talked with agreed to participate with the program development.

The first area we targeted was China.

As part of the program development, we asked each of the companies to grant us access to their Chinese employees so that we find out if we were meeting the needs of the local employees as well as the American businesses. On our side we also hired permanent employees in Beijing and Shanghai. To gain credibility, I knew we had to move faster than government was normally used too. We didn't see the need to rush, rather to just be more efficient, remove layers of hierarchy and provide decision authority within the leadership of the Chinese delegation. Within 6 months we were up and running, a monumental achievement. I had thought it would take at least a year to have a functional office open.

The beauty of our new, three-pronged methodology to implement this program became the foundation for government operations. The pillars of 1) no hierarchy, 2) give decision authority, and 3) remove bureaucratic process, led to a period of development that had likely never been seen before in government. In six months we had two working offices open, a market data web-site (in English and Mandarin), over 45 multi-sector experts on staff and had scheduled our first cultural seminar for US business people who would be working in China and dealing with operational issues. We also had expansion plans to open offices in six more cities, had started negotiations with local universities to create shared learning programs and were producing materials for distribution in America for smaller companies that might want to do business in China, but did not have the requirement for physical operations or a relocation to China. It was amazing.

The partner businesses that had collaborated with us to establish the office and to provide advice were immediately taking advantage of this service to get a competitive advantage, not only against their American counterparts but also against existing local and foreign national companies.

We offered guidance allowing American companies to enter the market quickly and without a steep learning curve. We provided market insight, important connections, databases, real estate advice, research programs, staff training, hiring opportunities and probably more statistics than anyone other than Chinese government itself. For once, business welcomed the government into their midst, but as a partner rather than as a regulator. A new and extraordinary collaborative and service-oriented role was born for government.

CHAPTER 10

A RELIGIOUS REFORMATION?...
ISLAM AND CHRISTIANITY

One of the formidable challenges facing globalization during my term as president was the emergence of Islam. As Islam spread into the western world, many nations had to look at their definitions of freedom and what that meant for the future of their nation.

As an American, it was clear that intent of the Founding Fathers was to ensure that religious freedom was an inalienable human right. I wholeheartedly agree with this. Let's face it: many of the early American settlers wanted to be in America so that they had freedom to worship as they chose without the fear of prosecution. Europe for centuries had not tolerated religious freedom and often even the suggestion of opposition to the church meant punishment or death. The First amendment to the Constitution reads:

> *Congress shall make no law respecting an establishment of religion, or prohibiting the free exercise thereof; or abridging the freedom of speech, or of the press; or the right of the people peaceably to assemble, and to petition the Government for a redress of grievances.*

Over time, this provision, which limited only the federal government, has been extended to each of the 52 states of the Union.

The Bill of Rights is not only a fantastic piece of American heritage, it is also the foundation of what we stand for.

Therefore, it was with unequivocal support that I was in favor of Islam being an accepted religion and that its followers were entitled to establish and practice in the United States of America. Opposition to Islam was generally a result of prejudice and fear on behalf of individual citizens and a few specific organizations.

In defense of Americans opposed to Islam at the time, and of course there is opposition even today, many had gained knowledge of Islam solely from the activities of ISIS and the aftermath of 9/11. The result was an attitude tainted with hate, maliciousness and of course resentment. This is entirely understandable, as I was horrified by the events of 9/11 and terrorists acts by ISIS. Yet on a personal level I had spent a lot of time in places like Indonesia and Northern Africa so I was familiar with Islam and the teaching of the Quran and I knew what happened in New York City and the actions of ISIS were attacks by terrorists rather than Muslims.

The second thing that heightened concerns was Turkey being granted "candidacy" into the European Union in 2006. Turkey is primarily a Muslim nation, which in and of itself is no concern, but Europe is a Christian-based region embracing western traditions of freedom, secular government and capitalism. Turkey as a society embraced these traits to a much lesser extent.

The three prime components of membership in the EU are the adoption of the Euro, the joining of a free-trade area and the ability of individuals to move freely throughout the Union. It this third component that worried me the most, and even today I am puzzled that others did not see the coming conflicts as Turkey provided a gateway to Europe for the spread of Islam.

Per the first amendment of the Constitution, the second tenet of US culture that deals with religion is the acknowledged separation of church and state. This had been clearly established through Supreme Court rulings as far back as the mid-1800s, stating that the federal government shall not be influenced by religion. In the mid-1900s, this same thought was extended to the state level by limiting the ability of state governments to promote one religion over another.

The "Dilemma of Islam," as I referred to it in 2017, was that for the first time in our history, there was a substantial group of Americans who felt that their religious beliefs required a government in accordance with religious doctrine.

The issue was a complicated one. Could religious freedom, by its very presence, lead to a reformation of the philosophies that our nation was founded upon? Hypothetically, allowing Muslims to enter society was permitting them to become politically powerful enough to change the fundamental nature of America. Though this may be seen as merely a theoretical discussion, I felt it necessary to explore the issue and to establish guidelines.

In 2012, British information showed that within the Islamic community over 40% of Muslims residents indicated that they would like to see Sharia Law imposed. This number clearly articulates the point for the future, that if Islamic groups were to gain any type of organizational strength and find their way into the political process, then it is not unreasonable to assume that there could be a fundamental shift in direction. In 2016, the city of London elected a Mulsim mayor, albeit one born and educated in Britain. Mr. Khan of course turned out to be an exemplary role-model and representative for the city.

The First Amendment of the Constitution offers religious freedom as a fundamental right of Americans. However, the dilemma is obvious. If those claiming religious freedoms are not interpreting that doctrine in a manner consistent with individual freedom, but rather profess a moral code and political direction that undermines the basic philosophy of individual freedom, then should it be opposed? I would say, unequivocally, yes.

Religious fundamentals are not universally shared, but the basis of America's origin was in the desire for individual freedom and an ability to make independent decisions. Any group or organization that disagrees with this view needs to be resisted.

At the time, people claimed that there should be a ban on Muslims entering the country, an action that would not be in keeping with the spirit of the USA. Presidential candidate Donald Trump had made the ban on Muslims a keystone of his campaign. There are groups that look to the US for the ideals of freedom and relief from persecution, so should our goals be to keep out the very people out who strive to partake in our world?

Secondly, Muslims are able to worship as they choose. They can build mosques, celebrate their holy days, and believe in Mohamed. It is not up to America to tell these people that they cannot believe in their deity any more than it is for Christians to force their views on their neighbors.

Where we were able to make ground-breaking guidelines, which ultimately became accepted practices, was through curtailing members of Islam from gaining any type of influence within the political process. Eventually, this thinking came to extend to all religious factions and what was considered a nebulous concept of separation of church and state, became a real hallmark of the American political process.

Many argued that this was a subversion of our core principles, one directed towards Christians. I included Christians in all aspects of my discussions, feeling equally opposed to Christianity in government, but I did not feel America would have to abandon its roots or even disassociate itself from the Christian religion by imposing universal guidelines. The basic enhancement was essentially this; At the political level, favoring one's personal religious affiliation over another's, and having the intent of imposing one's views on another, through policy, is not permitted.

This concept has become a benchmark in the modern world.

However, in 2018, the debate had clarified itself well enough that we were able to take several steps to curtail any emergent political movement that supported Sharia Law or other movements that might strive to change the nature of America. In addition to the Christian-bashing sentiment I endured, there were many critics who characterized these actions as prejudicial, that Muslims were being singled out. This was an accurate statement in terms of Muslims being the focal point, but the actions that were taken were in no way prejudicial. The basic sentiment was that America was a free country, but anyone who argued this and specifically wanted to move America away from this position of freedom would not be able to access the instruments of government.

The first of the principles was the outright banning of any immigrant Muslim from holding political office at any level until 2025. Two, the limiting of mobility within the nation's borders upon entry for a period of five years. Thirdly, the holding back of US citizenship until individuals had demonstrated an ability to abide the principles of the USA, and finally an outright ban on Muslim schools.

Though these principles might sound counter-intuitive to the basic fundamentals that the US holds paramount, keep in mind that America has only ever had to deal with fundamental opposition to individual freedom on this scale once before and that led to the Civil War. The goal of these actions was not to limit individual freedoms, rather to ensure that the thinking and principles that have allowed the United States of America to thrive continued. At an individual level, freedom was still the driving force.

The success of this initiative was predicated on the simple fact that any Muslim could worship freely. As the world knows now, Islam is not fundamentally the evil empire that it was portrayed to be 40 years ago. The vast majority of believers are citizens with unequivocal pride and loyalty to the USA. However, many Muslims do see a role for a religious-directed government. This situation warrants that there have to be limitations placed on groups that think this way.

America is still the "melting pot" of the world. You do not move to America and not become an American and embrace the values of freedom and democracy. It is as straightforward as that from a philosophical standpoint. Americans believe this and above all else hold that notion sacred.

One of the original tactics we developed as part of our government policies through "3POI-P", was that we reached an agreement with Canada that allowed easy emigration of any Muslim who did not agree with the principles. This was not so much a "love it or leave it" type of approach as it was more of a belief that freedom is a hallmark of the American way. As president, the last thing I wanted to do was force any individual citizen to live in a place that they did not want to.

We felt this was an extremely fair and reasonable first-step approach, as Canada offers a similar standard of living. Canada also has a decidedly different approach to religion. They have more of a multicultural society in which one can build a world unique to your culture if you so choose. The Canadian government will accommodate your individual beliefs and customs much more so than here in America. For an example, the Royal Canadian Mounted Police changed their uniform guidelines to accommodate Sikh religious paraphernalia such as turbans and ceremonial daggers. This would not ever happen in the USA.

Of course, anyone who had real issues with these guidelines had the right to head elsewhere in the world. As President, you sometimes have to draw clear lines so that people know what their options are. As suggested, all we were doing was imposing limitations on access to institutional levels of government and the political process. There was no hindrance of any individual's right to worship as they chose. This was to be the new law of the land.

Ironically, the issue has never been challenged by a Muslim. As I fervently argued, the vast majority of Muslims were no different than anyone else in America. They wanted to live in a part of the world whereby they could worship freely and live a comfortable life and raise their families in relative peace and security.

Of course, like any other religion, they do indeed have fundamentalists who hold an one-dimensional view of the world and these are the people and organizations that the legislation was designed to keep from gaining any type of authority and influence. In any case, in a democratic environment it is extremely difficult for people of that ilk to receive enough support to ever get into a role of influence anyway.

In Canada, where they are much more open to religious culture, there have been no instances of Muslims trying to change the nature of government. Unlike in the US, however, they have many Muslims in their Parliament and several cities have Muslims as their mayors. What people tend to forget is that most people adapt to their world rather than the other way around. The majority of people want to go about their day and are not motivated to get involved at a broader level. In America however, we hold a much more singular view of our nation and over the years have fought wars to defend it.

It somewhat goes back to the initial assertions that individual valuations be about money rather than personal characteristics. In the instance of the Muslim growth in America, only the specific individuals who had gained their wealth as well-deserving members of society would have been listened to and the rest would not have been considered anything to be worried about. It really is basic understanding of human nature, and the ability to distance one's self from evaluating people for biological or philosophical reasons.

Ironically, a major unintended consequence of the limitation imposed on Muslims was the decline of organized Christian religions in the United States. Though many churches still exist today at a community level, and are growing stronger all the time in terms of social issues and compassionate aid, at the organizational level in America they are virtually non-existent.

The Roman Catholic Church is virtually gone now as is the Protestant Church. The Vatican does not keep any emissaries or politicians in the US. Any form of organization is there primarily to facilitate the operation of the churches and to oversee community development.

The formalized version of religion has reverted to its original intent of creating a spiritual place for people to find comfort and to assist those who are in need of assistance after suffering hardship, a major advancement in the policy of the church and a fundamental service for many citizens.

The Evangelical churches, however, have grown and grown as modern worshipers strive to create personal relationships with God that are far beyond the parameters of traditional religious principles of obedience, sin and personal sacrifice.

I was genuinely inspired by the growth of Evangelical communities after we instituted the taxation measures. I openly admit that I was skeptical that many of the congregations would continue, and I'll admit to being jaded, seeing religion as merely a money-printing machine due to the tax-free status. As I pointed out earlier, I was maybe too cynical, and in hindsight I regret this, as well as some of the attitudes that I held regarding people's intentions. I have spent many years since apologizing and even making personal restitution for my lack of consideration and belief in other people's actions and intentions.

I think my position all stems from my need to control the world around me to the extent that I can. I know that what I am able to see and make happen is decidedly different from others. But I do not look at it as if I have received a gift from God; it is just who I am. Many can argue that who you are is simply what God made you, but I don't see it that way.

I do consider myself a spiritual being but not so much one who believes in religion. I have always felt that it is unnecessary to have to go to a building once a week to express my admiration for the world or revel in the spiritually of the earth. You can do that all on your own if you choose.

The main thing about organized religion though is that other people, regardless of their best intentions, tell their followers how to live their life, and in the worst-case scenario, what to do. I hold one principle sacred, and that is individual freedom. We all have the right to do as we want, whenever we want, but tempered with consideration for others. Religion undermines this principle and provides a set of rules and guidelines to follow. The one thing that I can never comprehend is why would anyone follow religious rules, and how would you know which one is the correct one to follow?

I have had first-hand experience with almost every type of religion in the world. The only one with meaning to me is Buddhism, just because it purports a fierce independence as well as a connection with the environment around you. The notion of karma originates in Buddhism, and I truly agree with this concept though I articulate it differently, seeing it as the effort you put in is the result you get back. Also, Buddhism has the concept of the eightfold path, which I agree with, though I see it simply as what you choose to participate in and focus on in life.

My fundamental problem with Christianity is the premise that we are burdened with the stigma of original sin and must spend the balance of our life atoning. This is a fundamental error in thinking, and deprives many people of ability to function fully in life as well as to achieve their potential, whereas I have the exact opposite view: people are born with unlimited capability and should strive to achieve their fullest potential. This is inherent in the American Dream, and I have always felt a bit of a paradox that America would be founded upon a notion of inherent frailty and weakness.

The other unappealing element of Christianity is the necessity to judge and convert others. Even in our enlightened world there are people who protest against same sex marriage, who threaten hospitals where abortions are performed and continue to adhere to outdated gender roles. I defend the individualist nature for one to believe whatever they want, but not as much when negativity is involved and it extends as far as physical threats against others. In these circumstances, Christians are nothing more than bullies. Fortunately in 2050 few people listen to these extremists.

Forgiveness and equality were never concepts that I held dear, and if you remember the story of Mr. Zahan and his attempt on my life back in 2016, then you'll recall my thinking.

Up until the attempt on my life I believed that humanity was equal by the standards of the United Nations. I did, however, hold some deep reservations that everyone was actually equal in terms of contribution to society and of value to others on an individual level. The sole determinant of equality should not be the fact that you biologically exist.

But the one area where I do fully believe there should be equality is in terms of access. Every individual should have access to the ability to earn a living. Every individual should have access to basic health care and medicine. Every individual should have access to clean water, food and shelter. Every individual should have access to free movement around the globe. These are principles I hold dear.

I do not look at these as innate rights, but rather ones that we as evolved citizens of the US should strive for, not only for our fellow Americans but for people around the globe. Everyone, once basic needs are taken care of, now has the ability to live where they want to live and how they want to live. They must find their own way, which to me is the true life experience. Of course, even now, as we look forward to the 22nd century, there are still parts of the world that have to improve in these areas.

My final and most salient issue with Christianity is the notion of forgiveness. As I have mentioned at numerous points and cited several examples, the single biggest reason why the US was where it was at the start of the 21st century was due to the complete lack of individual accountability and the willingness of society in general to overlook anti-social behavior. When you live in a world of free action, without shared direction or individual consequence, then it is inevitable that chaos in some measure will result and society will deteriorate.

At the start of the 21st century, there was no criminal accountability, financial sectors were for all intents and purposes unregulated, government was mostly ethically bankrupt, and we lived in a world where the ends justified the means. As long as the end warranted some financial gain then there was little chance that anyone would face any type of punishment. In fact, if you were indeed wealthy enough, your deviant behavior would likely bring you financial rewards due to the media coverage that you would receive and in all likelihood the subsequent book and movie. The bottom line was, that if you could make yourself or someone else money, you were likely to be forgiven. This was the direct result of the Christian ethic.

Religious fervor to absolve sins through confession rites lays the foundation for anyone to do anything they want, knowing full well that in the eyes of "their Lord" their action will be forgiven. Earthly punishments are mitigated as deterrents, regardless of the horrific nature of the person's actions. To me, this is a fundamentally unacceptable principle and one that I cannot embrace.

Now this does not mean that I do not share Christian values. The tenets of Christianity that revolve around love your neighbor and honesty and respect for your family, are all worthy, and are ones I hold dearly in my heart as do most Americans. My critics over the years have objected strongly to my views on religion, and that is perfectly fine. My opinions, however, were always based on finding a reasonable way to make an assessment of someone, rather than an emotional one based on a lack of knowledge, or by fear.

I prefer to take a compassionate approach, to consider the impact and the residual effects that any policy might lead too. Concepts of forgiveness and equality are easily exploited by the hateful, so extreme diligence and communication was required when developing policy.

The result was that the American population grew together and as a result, there was vastly more self-policing by society at large than there had ever been before. This shared view of America enabled the nation to move beyond the petty squabbles of the period and shifted people toward an action-oriented agenda rather than one of restriction and limitation against others.

This ability to be accommodating when everyone is in a positive frame of mind is what makes America great and powerful. What individuals mostly care about is how your actions and thinking will impact upon them but when we as a nation get together to move forward on an issue, there are now institutional guidelines and infrastructure in place to make it happen, and nothing is beyond our ability to get it done.

CHAPTER 11

THOUGHTS FOR MY CRITICS

So how do I like being referred to the Founding Father of the 21st Century or ff21st?

To be honest, I feel more and more comfortable with it every day. I have come to realize, over time, that the personal accolades that I have received are not so much a result of bravado or an attempt to single me out, but rather recognition by other Americans for my contribution to our country. As I get older, I can look back and see why ff21st is now a more plausible designation than I could at other points in my life.

One amusing thing about being president is that even though I worked and lived right on the Washington Mall, I never once truly walked around it and absorbed the significance of the area. I had previously been to the Mall during a field trip in high school, but at the time I was more enamored with the Smithsonian Museums than any of the historical monuments.

So finally, in 2028, I made a point of visiting the Mall and walking the entire area.

You know what struck me the most? That our historical monuments were made up of two things: the first was esteemed visionary people, and the second was war.

And now there are plans to build a pavilion to me upon my death. I have refused to be part of any development while I am alive. I figure a monument of that sort is entirely up to the

American people and something that I should be no part of. To be involved in the building of a monument to myself sounds terribly egotistical.

I am also now more comfortable being included in a group with presidents like George Washington, Thomas Jefferson and Abraham Lincoln. Washington and Jefferson, two of the original founding fathers of our nation, provided the thought-leadership and foundation for what the country was to become. President Lincoln, though not a founding father, was instrumental in holding the country together through the most difficult period in our history.

Myself, I feel I am getting credit for showing a new way forward that addressed the complexity of the 21st century. More importantly, I think what I did was remind people of what it is to be American, and that ultimately led to cultural shifts. I don't feel like I did anything brilliant like my predecessors, rather I just put the country back on track. Others had gotten so muddled and self-centered in their approach that they forgot they were Americans first and foremost. If that deserves recognition then so be it. I am happy that I could contribute.

The moniker of ff21st is a tribute to the respect that America has toward me, and this is the first time I have ever used it. Personally, I like being called Henderson but even Natalie on occasion calls me "Twenty-one." Fortunately, Jimmy just calls me Dad, which is my favorite title.

I have a few closing words to say to my many critics in the United States and around the world. First off, thank you for existing and for putting forward opposition during my term as president. Opposition leads one to be much more thorough and to consider points of view that may not have otherwise entered the debate.

For those critics who despise me due to the fact that I perhaps changed their notion of what America should be, then all I can do is state that I believe in a democratic and free America. The vast majority of Americans are thrilled with the advancements and the state of our Union as we head into the latter half of the 21st century. Therefore, though I defend your right to hold an opinion I also choose to dismiss it. You of course can protest, write letters and attempt to undermine me at every step of the way – that is your right as an American. My right, I feel, even when I was president, is to acknowledge, but ignore you. If I am wrong in that approach, then the "Engaged Democracy" model will make sure that your issues will come to the surface and be dealt with. If they do not, then that essentially means that too few people consider them as relevant.

To the critics who are more fantastic in their hopes and dreams and felt that I never went far enough for the United States, or on occasion that I took a path that was anti-human rights, I suggest that you please keep shooting for perfection and envisioning your personal ideal. One of the on-going critiques throughout my presidency was that I was always too practical and political in my policies and actions.

Both of these statements are potentially accurate but not completely true.

One of my underlying thoughts in life was that it is nearly impossible to go from zero to 100. I called this the "magic wand" approach, and idealists tend to expect a perfect world based on humanity first and everything else second. Many people hold the expectation that people can just wave their hands and everything will be different. I do not think there is any scenario in the world where this applies and certainly it does not at a national level. I feel it is absolutely necessary to move in the right direction, but like anything else it takes time to get there. There are two reasons why we will never reach such an ideal place. First: there is no ideal without everyone agreeing on what that ideal is; and secondly, our concept of ideal today is unlikely to be the ideal in the future. Idealism is a fluid concept based on people, context and perspective.

The analogy I've used most often to explain idealism is weight loss. If you weigh 200 lbs and want to get to 150 but you also want to have six-pack abs as your ideal, you do not simply go to bed, wake up the next day and the weight is gone. There is a whole series of steps to reaching your goal. The first of course, and this is the most important, is that you have an entirely different attitude about your health, body and mind. Deciding to not pick up that bag of potato chips is a basic tactic but does nothing in the long-term. The reality is that your ideal appearance has to be something you want, and then you develop a plan and execute with discipline. Of course, the final step is the internalizing of the new mindset forever into the future as a means of solidifying your goal. If not, there is always the chance you'll revert to the previous ways. Diligence and perseverance are as important as visionary thinking.

The simplicity of any planning process is that there are short-term targets that are easily attainable and too many people get excited about these achievements early on. For example, with the dieting analogy, the obvious step is to cut out all the sugar-based products like soda, candy, pastries and chips. Well, anyone can make that decision and within a week will have dropped a few pounds. This gives them the comfort, results and motivation to continue for a few more weeks and in the first 30 days you lose ten pounds. This is great, and most people would be pretty happy to have this.

Of course, the real hurdle is how to get beyond ten pounds. Continuing to cut out sugar-based products will not get you much further. Now, there is the whole issue of exercise, eating proper nutritious meals, stress reduction and all the other things we know that can contribute to overall health and weight loss.

I can imagine that once have stayed stable at the ten pound weight loss you will be less motivated to achieve your stated goal. There will be moments of weakness and before too long soda, candy, pastry and potato chips are back in your life. Even if you maintain the ten pound weight loss you are still nowhere near your goal of losing 50 pounds. Without a complete commitment to healthy living, the goal is impossible. It is easy to become complacent and be satisfied with partial results.

Now, in order to obtain the six-pack abs is a whole different level of accomplishment and will likely require you to change your life and not just your nutritional habits. To get to this level you not only have to exercise regularly but you have to change the people you associate with, especially the friends with bad habits, and replace them with a group of people who are totally committed to fitness.

Now, imagine that you decided that your individual weight-loss goal was to be achieved by your entire family. Though that is a great and ambitious goal you can easily imagine the difficulties. Now, keep expanding that dream to your neighbors, your community, your entire town and you get the idea of the challenges in getting anywhere significantly in a short period of time. This is the challenge I faced every day in changing the mindset of Americans.

Changing attitudes and culture is the only way to make lasting progress and, unfortunately, this takes time. Attitudinal shifts do, however, deliver significant and lasting results.

Therefore, many of the approaches that I took in the early days appeared to have minimal impact on our country but eventually delivered. Secondly, and this is most important, is that the efforts being made were to change the attitude of a large group of people rather than leaving it up to a few people to lead the changes. There was no progress for America with only a small portion of the population embracing the thinking. The bottom line was that we had to have a shared consciousness and common goals in order to regain our strength as a nation.

Hence, the "magic wand" just does not exist, especially on a broad scale, and idealism is something that has to be a lofty vision rather than a tangible result.

Many people have critiqued my usage of money as the benevolent tool to guide America. There were multitudes of claims that this line of thinking stemmed strictly from my individual wealth and I'm sure on some level this might have been true, at least initially. I doubt I would have ever had the opportunity to do the things I did if I had not been a successful businessman. However, that was just the way it was; I did not ask to be president, it just sort of happened.

I have never stated these comments so boldly but here goes. America is about money. Period.

To ignore this fact is to ignore the basis of what America is all about.

The United States of America was founded by a merchant class who wanted to escape Europe because they could not achieve any formal political authority in the existing monarchical systems. They had the wealth and wanted more influence. They were tired of being persecuted and essentially robbed for being wealthy.

The fact that this group of people went out of their way to create the United States is testament to the desire they had to create a nation that represented their vision. To abandon this motivational force is un-American.

Some have even argued that my desire to place money at the forefront of the human condition is tantamount to being the voice of Satan himself. Now that is clearly ridiculous, but I can understand it. Almost everyone believes we should be driven by an innate compassion towards the betterment of the human condition. I too would like to see nothing more than the entirety of humanity operate in this fashion. However, I have not yet seen the evidence that as human beings we have the capacity or capability to do this. I do expect that, at some point in the far distant future, humanity will be naturally peaceful, but in 2050 it is still not part of our collective DNA. We have just not evolved that far yet though many of us know that it is good to be compassionate.

Let's face it, we are a young, evolving species, and through that time we have done a tremendous amount of killing of each other and have gone to extreme lengths to protect our property or impose our wishes. This is the innate nature of man. Once you recognize this fact of humanity it is much easier to deal with rather than holding out hope that some other characteristic will miraculously emerge. The problem with hope for humanity is that you are continuously disappointed.

My view of humanity, however, does not necessarily have to be construed as negative or as a comment on the moral failure of humans, rather just a step in the process of our development.

My goal in the absence of common or even compassionate human values was to utilize money as the guiding force.

The one common denominator that I have been able to identify in my lifetime is the universal appeal and power of money and the desire for individuals to accumulate it. Many can argue that money is the "root of all evil" but that is a flawed concept. Money is the root of all development, longevity and prosperity. How money is utilized can be debated to the end of time, but the influence of money has transformed the world in less than 150 years to be a much more equitable global community.

Too many people want the world to be happy and peaceful without considering or taking the necessary steps to get there. This is a foolish approach when you consider it. How was the world going to go from the corruptness, violence and selfishness of 2016 to a peaceful, compassionate and honest place without starting to move in that direction? It is easy to say that this is the way the world should be, but without any substance on how to get there it is just a platitude. Money did not lead America to be devoid of these basic principles, people did.

Despite the criticism, what I feel I have done above all else is identify the path forward and take steps towards a loftier vision. Money was simply the tool to lead us in that direction.

A third area where I received criticism is my tolerance of existing institutions. Though I despised most of them in my youth, it is nonetheless necessary to build on the existing foundation. Many critics are quick to call for a new way to do things, but it is impossible and wasteful to start over. The fact is, established institutions should be utilized into the future. The best example from my days as president was democracy and the instruments of government.

Prior to the election in 2016 there were many people calling for a whole new system of government and even the elimination of Congress. This situation existed despite the best efforts of President Barack Obama, whose motivations were generally in the spirit of the American Way and hope. The American political and business system was so decadent and mischievous that leadership became inherently untrustworthy by simply being a part of it. In my business dealings I was pretty much a lone exception.

The events of 2011-2015 led to the downfall of President Obama. He was not ineffective, but people became disappointed of hearing how he was unable to exert any influence over the system that he had claimed he would reform. By the time the election was held in 2016, he had drifted so far from his original positions, ones that had swept him to power in 2008, that he was barely recognizable. He was still the same person but that he had abandoned most of his beliefs in return for expediency. His biggest failure though had been cooperation with the Republican Party after the Republicans had taken over Congress in the 2010 mid-term elections. President Obama started to realize that expediency usurped vision, and as a result, he was doomed to failure. As I have said many times, President Obama was indeed the right person but at the wrong time. He was just incapable of standing up for America and delivering an appropriate platform for the future versus short-term and political interests. It was a real shame.

In 2015, trust in Congress had dropped to below 10% and I fully agreed that Congress and the political system were ineffective, but the popular movement to burn Capitol Hill to the ground in 2017 and just rebuild was ludicrous. I was shocked that so many citizens had gotten behind that idea, but it was testament to just how disillusioned many Americans had become.

President Obama had been limited by the nature of politics not democracy itself. What people at the time were incapable of doing was looking for new ways to move forward and to break the log jam that the party system had constructed. I guess, in hindsight, this might have been my strength. Where others could not find a way through the system, I was always capable of looking at the system and seeing how to recreate it. Hence 3POI-P and the emergence of "Engaged Democracy" as the model to replace the representative system.

Leadership required observation and clarity rather than brilliance.

The Occupy movement was not simply a frustrated cry for a new government by the disenfranchised and disillusioned. What was actually being called for was an enhanced role in the political process and I could see that these people just wanted to feel like Americans again. I capitalized on that feeling.

All through the recessionary period leading up to my election in 2016, too many people had been economically affected and felt that America wasn't strong anymore. This feeling hit them at a personal level, and I think it called into question what it meant to be an American. When they demanded attention through protests, they were dismissed or called malcontents by a group of elitist government and economic higher-ups. The fact that they were not listened to and were on occasion forcibly assaulted by police further alienated them from America.

I recognized this and was able to provide a common mindset, and through valuable restructuring efforts such as the "New Freedom Initiative" and the "People, Politics, Position of Interest" (3POI-P) people began to feel engaged and positive about their role as American citizens again. This was key to whatever transpired during my term and has since continued. Americans now have a sense of what they are working towards and how they can contribute to keeping us a leading nation, a feeling that has been lost by the preceding generation, the entitled and selfish Boomer generation that brought America to the brink of inconsequence.

The birth of "Engaged Democracy" could never have occurred without the foundation being laid for a more inclusive democracy.

I am happy to state that as we are surpass the year 2050, America is more powerful than ever and is the world's thought-leader again. The world continues to move in a direction of economic growth, peaceful times, an improved standard of living. The result is a healthier and cooperative world.

America to me represents all that is good in humanity, a nation that fosters and encourages the true spirit of the human condition. I am thrilled, to say the least, that I have contributed to this development.

God Bless America!

AUTHOR'S NOTE

Founding Father of the Twenty-First Century is a work of fiction. While drawing on current American and world events I have made very little effort to provide complete or even accurate information. I have made many presumptions regarding the attitudes of individuals referenced and the circumstances described.

Though many real people are referenced in this work, the assertions are the views of the author only and represent my unique perspective. To do this I have created a "reality" specific to this work. I have further invented characters, extended real people into imagined situations and invented American and world events.

This book makes no claim to be literal truth nor do I set out to offend any person, group, organization or nation. The goal of this work is to provoke thought and propose alternatives for a better form of democracy. The ultimate hope is that a dialogue can begin to shape a better future. I hope that it has met this objective for you.

Henderson West is on the net:
Web-site   www.ff21st.com
                www.engaged-democracy.com
Facebook   Engaged Democracy
Twitter   @ff21st

Or, contact the author by e-mail:
kennethjackson@engaged-democracy.com

Printed in the United States
By Bookmasters